THE
OUTLAW ISLAND

A Novel

D. N. Bedeker

Cover photo by Janet Bedeker
Cover & book design by Jon Michael Miller

Other Books by D. N. Bedeker

The Cassidy Posse

Dark Hearts, White City

Hot Pursuit in Paradise

ACKNOWLEDGEMENTS

I would like to express my appreciation to Robin Adkins of the Chipman Library for all her help with research and Sue Kerkstra for her valuable input. Also Nancy Porter for sending me pictures of old Momence and keeping me straight on what businesses were around in 1867. Many thanks to Denise Wessman and Jimmy Carter for sharing their knowledge of the Kankakee River. A special thanks to Charles Hess, great grandson of Jake Hess, for reading the book and helping with the depiction of the Hess Family.

A huge measure of gratitude to author Jon Michael Miller ("Professor Mike") for helping with editing and formatting. Many thanks to the rest of the Dunedin Writers for their input and support.

And I must thank my wife Janet for her support and my grandson Danny for letting me into the mind of a twelve-year-old.

~

AUTHOR'S NOTES

The inspiration for this novel began with a text from my friend Dan Buchler who informed me there was a show on PBS about the Everglades. I spend the winters in Florida and have become interested in the preservation of "the Glades" as they are commonly known. When I began watching the PBS show, "Everglades of the North," I realized it was about an entirely different area. The topic being presented was about the Grand Kankakee Marsh and a large lake that once existed there.

I had heard years ago that there was once a marsh south of my home in Northwest Indiana, but I had never heard of a large lake, measuring six by eight miles, that once existed there. During the summer my family had a camper at Indiana Beach and we have travelled down route 41 many times without realizing we were driving across what was once Beaver Lake. I was shocked to find out this impressive body of water was drained in 1872 to create more farmland. This was made possible by the Swamplands Act of 1850 that turned all Federal swamp areas over to the states where they existed with the requirement that they be turned into arable farmland.

In doing research for my first book, *The Cassidy Posse*, I visited the famous "Hole in the Wall" in Wyoming and other outlaw hangouts without ever suspecting that one of the first was twenty miles south of my home in Indiana. In the middle of Beaver Lake was an island of horse thieves and counterfeiters known as Bogus Island. The most infamous criminal to frequent the island went by the name of Mike Shafer. He was a cutthroat who ruled the outlaw swamp country for several decades.

~

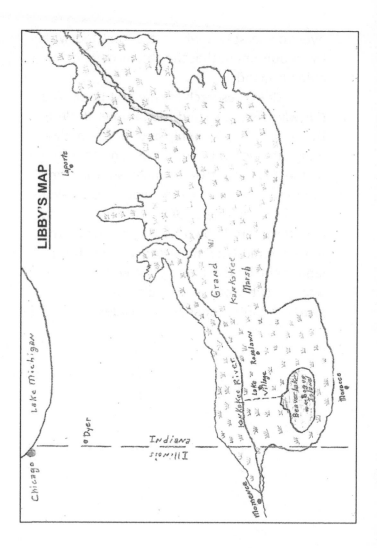

LIBBY'S MAP

PROLOGUE
Momence, Illinois, 1867

"The stallion is in the last stall."

"What are we taking besides the stallion?" asks the man holding the kerosene lantern. The soft glow of the light illuminates his hardened features. He is unshaven and long strands of gray hair escape from underneath his rebel hat.

"I told you to get rid of that hat. The war is over. All we can do now is take anything we can get from these Yanks."

"Okay, Sarge, that's what I was asking. What are we taking besides the stallion?"

"Take the sorrel mare. She's easy to ride and the stallion will trail behind her."

"What's Skeeter gonna ride?"

"Where is Skeeter?"

"Right here, Sarge." A small hunched man appears from the shadows. He drags his left foot as he walks.

"Skeeter, put a bridle on that dappled-gray filly. She'll bring a good price. You ride her and trail that Shetland pony. The Major says there's a good market for those back East. Rich little Yankee kids love 'em."

"Bill's afraid to put a halter on that stallion," chides Skeeter. "That big, black devil nipped him a good one."

"I'm not afraid of any horse," Bill counters angrily.

"I'll help you get a bridle on him," says Sarge. "I got a spaded bit that will hurt like hell if he gets too frisky."

The two men corner the big horse in his stall and manage to get the bridle on him. Skeeter mounts the dappled gray and is the first out of the stable and into the moonlight; he pulls the pony behind him. When Bill rides on the mare, the stallion does not follow docilely, even with the restrictive bit in his mouth. He snorts and rears up in the corral outside the stable. The Sarge sees a lamp being lit in an upstairs window.

"Okay, get going," says the Sarge. "We musta woke the widow and her kid up."

The two men exit the open gate of the stable and turn east, heading for the Indiana state line and outlaw country.

~

CHAPTER 1
Horse Thieves in the Night

My name is Ben Tanner and I've been robbed. A few nights ago some fellows broke into our family's stable and stole three horses and a pony. I woke up when my mother yelled up the stairs that she heard noises outside. I real quick went to the window and threw it open. There was a sliver of a moon out, so I got a look at them, but not a good one. Two were kind of big and there was a little one that walked with a limp. I put on my pants and hurried downstairs, but by the time I got down there, they had disappeared into the night. I could tell by the hoofbeats they were headed east though, towards the Indiana border and outlaw country.

Tanner Stables has been here in Momence since the town's beginning in 1834. My father was the second generation, but he died in the great war between the states. He didn't die a hero's death in battle though. He died a slow, terrible death in a prison called Andersonville.

Since then my mother has been in a sad state of despair, not knowing what to do. My father was always very protective of her and said she was too sensitive and artistic to be part of running the stables. She wrote poetry and played the piano for us at night. I could tell he really loved her.

After we got the news of his death, I became the man of the family and took over the business. It's been hard for me being only twelve and I couldn't have done it without the help of my friend Eli Brown. He is fourteen and almost six feet tall; that's nearly a head taller than me. His grandfather used to work for us and taught him to be a farrier. Eli can shoe horses as well as anybody.

Still, folks in town were a little concerned about leaving their horses in the care of a couple of schoolboys. Business picked up a little when Frank took over. I hate to admit that because I really don't like Frank. He showed up here last fall and wished to pay his respects. He said he had served under my father, Captain Thomas Tanner, in Illinois's Fighting Forty-Second Infantry and that he heard my father died in Andersonville prison.

When my mother found out Frank had no job, she put him up in the bunkhouse where Eli's grandfather used to live. He was our new man in charge. I got along with him okay at first, but I could tell he was trying really hard to please my mother. Now, with spring here, he has become a regular at our dinner table. I guess my mother is an all right cook, but the way Frank goes on, you would think she could give the chefs in those fancy hotels in Chicago a run for their money. I figure his next move will be sleeping in the house.

When I really took a dislike to Frank is when he fired Eli. During the war and for more than a year after, me and Eli kept Tanner Stables going. There hasn't been one man in town ever complained about Eli shoeing his horse. His grandpappy did it for years for our family until he had a stroke back in '63 and couldn't work anymore.

Then somebody at the tavern uptown told Frank that Eli's grandfather was a negro. Frank's view of Eli changed after that. He said Eli worked too slow and wasn't doing a good job. No matter what Eli did, Frank would find some fault with it. Frank fired Eli and sweet talked my mother into going along with it. I didn't talk to either one of them for a week. I'm glad nobody told him that Eli's mother was part Indian. That would have set something else off I suppose.

Eli was a mix of so many things, you could not be sure of his race by just looking at him. He had a flat nose that looked like it had been punched a few times. It was set in the middle of a face framed with high cheekbones and a forehead that stuck out over his green eyes like an armor plate. He wore his straight black hair long and his skin was the color of cocoa.

He looked nothing like me, but he was my big brother. Now, that's not in the sense that we had the same parents. His were killed trying to protect slaves from bounty hunters that were following the Underground Railroad.

His grandfather, having no other place to take his grandson, brought him here to work with him when Eli was only three. They lived in our bunkhouse and Eli was there to help me learn to walk when I was a toddler. He has been there for me ever since.

Now I am standing here after sundown by the corner of the house waiting to talk to Eli about my plan.

"Ben, you here?"

I saw Eli peeking around the corner of the stable.

"Yeah, I'm over here behind the rain barrel."

"Is Mr. Frank around?"

"Naw. He's been going up to the tavern lately right after supper. Tells my ma he's drumming up new business."

Eli moved towards me after hearing this news.

"What good's new business goin' ta do him if'en he ain't got nobody ta shoe hosses?"

"He hired a guy yesterday. I think he met him in the tavern. He showed up smelling like whiskey this morning."

"He any good?"

"Don't know. Haven't seen him do anything yet."

"Hmm."

"Forget Frank for now. The problem is the sheriff."

"Why's he the problem?"

"Can't get him to do anything. Says he tracked those fellers to the Indiana state line so he can't go any farther. He says it's out of his jurisdiction. He told my ma those horses are probably on Bogus Island by now. No posse is going out there."

"What'd your ma say?"

"You know her. She just walked away and started crying. Then Frank put his arm around her and reassured her that nothing could be done. He wasn't any help at all. Now old man Tyler that owns the dappled gray filly says we are responsible. His horse was in our care. Now he is going to sue us for fifty dollars."

"Well, you lost the most. Didn't somebody offer your ma three hundred dollars fer Trooper?"

"Yeah, that was Mr. Hess. I had a tough time talking her out of doing it."

"Now why would a man give that much fer a hoss?"

"Because he saw you riding Trooper down River Street at a full gallop. Libby told me she heard Jake Hess talking to her dad. Mr. Hess said he didn't believe any horse in the county could stay with Trooper in a mile race."

"A mile race?"

"Why haven't you heard? In June they're having a big horse race on the road west of town."

"So? They're always havin' races west ah town. Usually quarter mile or half mile runs. Momence being ah sportin' town with all the trappers, hunters and teamsters passin' through, there's always drinkin' and gambling goin' on."

"Well, this is going to be different. They are trying to start a horse fair as an annual shindig. The purse for the race is going to be a thousand dollars."

Eli let out a low whistle. "A thousand dollars."

Now that I had impressed Eli, I thought it was a good time to make my pitch.

"Eli, we can't just do nothing and let those scallywags make off with Trooper. You and I were there when he was born. You remember how my dad and your grandfather had to pull on his legs to get him out he was so big. We can't sit here and do nothing now that he's been stolen."

"What are we gonna do if'en the grownups ain't doin' nothing?"

"I have a plan, but I don't want to tell you the whole thing out here standing in the dark. Can you stand on this rain barrel and climb up the drainpipe to the window of my room?"

"I suppose I could."

"Good. I'll go up and open the window. I'll haul you in."

CHAPTER 2
A Plan Takes Shape

When I got up the stairs to my room, Eli was already clinging to the downspout outside my window. I pulled him in headfirst and he sprawled onto my bedroom floor. The old straw hat he always wore fell off his head and he rolled over it, crushing it flat. We both started laughing, but I heard my mother coming up the stairs and we hushed. Eli snatched up his crumpled hat and jumped in the closet just before she stuck her head in my room.

"Benjamin, did I hear laughing up here?"

"Yes, Mother. It was I. Frank told me a funny joke and I was just thinking about it."

"Oh, well, I hope it was a decent sort of joke. Glad you two are getting along better. We need a man to run the stable. It's no job for a poor widow and a boy, you know."

"Yes, Mother." She looked at me as though there was something else she wanted to say, but didn't. "Good night, Ben."

When she closed the door, Eli stuck his head out to see if it was all clear. I motioned him over and we sat on the floor by my bed.

I lit the lamp so we could see each other as we talked.

"A funny joke Frank told ya," said Eli. "Now that's ah funny joke right there."

"Well, that's what she would like to hear. It's all part of learning to handle grown-ups."

"Oh, ya'll an expert on that, huh?"

"Yeah, I know some. You ever notice how I always talk in perfect grammar and diction to my ma?"

"How would I notice that? I don't even know what that stuff is."

"That's how Mr. Trowbridge taught us. If I don't talk like that, I have to hear how she wasted money sending me to him for private tutoring."

"Yeah, I remember you and Libby and ah few other rich kids in town were too good fer the little red schoolhouse. Well, you ain't rich no more so you'se can talk like everybody else."

"But if we could win that thousand dollars, we could be back in the money."

Eli pulled back and got a real skeptical look on his face. "What're ya thinkin'?"

"If we go to Bogus Island and get Trooper back, you can ride him in the big race and win the thousand dollars."

"That's it? That's yer big plan? You and me go to an island full ah growed up killers and hoss thieves and steal Trooper back."

"Well, I didn't say it was a great plan. What do you expect from a twelve-year-old?"

"You ain't got no plan at all. All's ya got is an idear. Now a plan needs a lot more thinkin' out. Ya gotta figure out what kind of provisions and what not you're gonna need. Then ya gotta figure the best way ta get there and how we can get Trooper back without gettin' killed."

Now unbeknownst to Eli, that was my plan all along. I knew if I could get him thinking about it, he would come up with a plan.

"So, can we leave tomorrow?" I asked.

"Heck, no. I gotta go back to Hopkins Park and get Miss Nelly to take care of my grandpappy. I'll get his shotgun too. He said he was going to give it to me cause he can't shoot no more."

"Shotgun," I said, surprised. Now some reality was beginning to settle in on me. "Are we going to shoot it out with these outlaws?"

"Heck, no. I need it to shoot us some birds or a rabbit to eat. We ain't gonna shoot it out with no gunmen."

I felt relieved to hear this, but it got me thinking. *What are we going to do?*

"We'll need a boat," declared Eli. "We can't get out to Bogus Island without a boat."

Okay, some details of the plan. It was as though Eli had read my mind.

"We can take our rowboat," I offered.

"It's the end of May," said Eli. "The river's too fast in the spring." He was leaning forward resting his chin in his hands, considering all the possibilities. "Too hard to row upstream. We need a canoe. It will cut through the water better."

"Libby has a canoe," I said. "We can borrow it. I'm sure she wouldn't mind."

"How you so sure she won't mind?"

"The red pony, Scarlett. She belongs to Libby."

"So now we're bringing back two hosses?"

"We'll bring back all four if we can."

"Hmm." Eli pondered this a moment. "That's ah real bold plan fer ah couple of young'uns like us ta pull off."

"We can do it. We'll have surprise on our side. Those outlaws won't expect anyone to come out there after them."

"You're right. They'd never expect an adult ta do something that dumb."

I thought I had better let that discouraging remark pass and get Eli focused on the plan.

"What do you want me to get besides the canoe?" I asked.

"Well, you'll need four good ropes outah the stable if'en you wanna try ta bring'em all back. That's gonna be tricky, trying ta get four hosses to swim off that island behind ah canoe in the middle of the night."

"In the middle of the night?"

"How else ya think we can sneak them off Bogus island?"

I tried to picture this, and it didn't seem too realistic, I had to admit. If we could just get Trooper and Libby's red pony, I'd be happy.

"If ya could scrounge up some farmer matches and ah compass, that'd help too," said Eli. "And go over ta Conrad Bakery and get us some hard bread."

"So how soon do you think we can leave?"

"Morning after next," he said as he crawled out the window. "I'll meet you at sunrise at where ya keep yer rowboat down at the dock."

I was so excited about what we were about to do, I knew I would not be able to fall asleep. I pulled out a stack of Beadle and Adams dime novels from under my bed and started reading *Old Bear Paw, the Trapper King.* The exciting cover showed the Trapper King fighting off a huge bear, and he was armed only with a Bowie knife. I suppose he had to make all these plans and figure out what supplies he was going to need before he went out on one of his adventures, but the book never mentioned it. I guess all those details would just slow down the story.

~

CHAPTER 3
Who's Going Along

I found Libby's canoe behind the Carter's outhouse and grabbed the rope on the bow to drag it down to the dock. That is when I saw Libby running towards me. When she skidded in next to me, her blonde hair was a tussled mess and the color was rising in her cheeks. She handed me a folded piece of paper and smiled.

"What's this?"

"It's a map. It's a map of the marsh. It will help us find Beaver Lake and this Bogus Island where they take stolen horses."

I took the piece of paper and spread it out on the bow of the canoe.

"How did you do this?"

"My father has all these parchment maps in his study. I just scaled it down."

"You sketched this?"

"He has a big map of the State of Indiana and I just traced this section so it's small enough to put in your pocket. I even put in a legend so we can judge distance."

By the legend, Indiana appeared to be about ten miles to the east. Once you crossed over the state line, Beaver Lake was about four or five miles south of the river. The lake itself was bigger than I thought. It was around six miles long going north to south and eight miles wide. Bogus Island was in the southwest part of the lake. The only town indicated was Lake Village on the northeast end of Beaver Lake.

"Ben, I want to go with you," she blurted out.

"Are you crazy? You're a girl!" I blurted back.

As soon as I said it, I knew that was the wrong thing to say to Libby. I should have been ready for it when I had heard an "us" when she spoke earlier, but I had paid it no mind.

"I'm a girl! What does that have to do with it?"

Well, it had everything to do with it. Folks would not think it was proper. I tried to remember some of Mr. Trowbridge's suggestions on being tactful and avoiding arguments. He once told me I had a very good vocabulary for my age. I was going to need it to climb out of this hole my big mouth had just dug for me.

"Libby, think about it. We are going into a swamp full of dangerous creatures, not to

17

mention ruthless outlaws. Proper folks would say that is not a place for a young lady. Now that's not me saying that, mind you."

"Then why did you even bring it up?"

I have known Elizabeth Cary Carter for as far back as I can remember. Since both of our fathers were officers in the Fighting 42nd Infantry, our families used to meet socially at least once a week. The women gossiped in the parlor while the men retired to the den and smoked cigars and had serious talks of war. That left plenty of time for Libby and me to get acquainted. We slipped outside and played with wooden guns that my father had carved for me. She liked to pretend we were with a wagon train on the Oregon Trail and were being attacked. Sometimes she would sneak out wearing pants just like a boy. I even smuggled her some I had outgrown.

"So just the two of you are going?' she asked, although I'm sure she already knew the answer.

"That's right. Just Eli and me."

"Eli and I," she corrected.

"Yeah, okay, Eli and I are going into the wilderness." I made a sweeping movement with my hand east towards the Grand Kanka- kee Marsh. "We could be gone for days.

We're going to have to hunt for our own food and survive off the land."

"Ben, you don't know any more about surviving off the land than I do."

"Maybe not, but Eli does. Before his grandfather had his stroke, they would go into the marsh overnight hunting and fishing. I would have gone, but my mother wouldn't let me."

"Then she certainly isn't going to give you permission to go into Indiana to try and get horses back from a gang of horse thieves."

"I'm not going to ask permission. That's why I told you to keep this a secret buried six feet deep. Eli says if there's something a guy's got to do, the only way around adults is to ask forgiveness, not permission."

"So, do whatever you want and then apologize later."

When Eli said it, it made me feel real manly, but when Libby put it like that, it didn't sound so good. Libby was always a master at getting me tripping over my own tongue and looking foolish. I decided to avoid further argument and take the coward's way out.

"I'll ask Eli about it. He's the leader of this expedition and he'll know more about what we are up against."

Libby looked at me skeptically. "You promise?"

"Yes, Yes, I'll ask him. Now help me tote this canoe down to the river so we are ready to go at daybreak tomorrow. Eli says it's important we get an early start. It's going to be hard to paddle against the current."

~

CHAPTER 4
Into the Wild

A mist hung over the water as Eli and I loaded the canoe the next morning. I brought the rope, two full canteens and my father's binoculars. My hope was we could see the bad guys before they saw us. Eli did not bring his grandpappy's shotgun because there were no shells and no money in the family to buy any. That removed hunting as a food supply, but his aunt made up for it by making a mess of corn dodgers.

I brought two loaves of hard bread from Conrad's Bakery, a frying pan and a fishing pole short enough to go into the canoe without being a bother. I also brought a trenching shovel to dig up worms and cover the fire. We might get ourselves killed in some other manner, but we would not starve.

"How much you got here?" asked Eli, lifting the coil of rope I had borrowed from the stable.

"About fifty feet."

"Don't knows if that'll be enough," he said, pushing back his beat-up straw hat.

"We might have to make lassos fer four hosses."

I wasn't that optimistic about recovering all four horses, so I didn't think it would be a problem.

"You want me to go back and find more rope?"

"Naw, jump in and let's get goin'," said Eli. "We gotta ways ta go today."

"Yeah, about ten miles upstream to the Indiana state line."

"Heard it was about eight."

"On Libby's map it looks like ten miles."

"Libby's Map?"

Then, like she had been waiting for her cue, I saw Libby running down the slope towards us. I don't know how she slipped out of the house at six in the morning, but I was now faced with the conversation I had wished to avoid.

"Ah, Eli, I forgot to ask you. Can Libby come along?"

The look I got was to be expected. "Heck, no. You know that." He looked at me a long moment before saying. "You puttin' me on the spot fer this, ain't ya, Ben?"

The sheepish look on my face answered the question for him.

Before Libby could reach us, Eli pushed the canoe off. We were twenty feet away from the shore when her momentum carried her into the water up to her knees.

"Ah, Libby, you can't go," I yelled. It came out sort of lame and indecisive, but I knew I had better not say that Eli said she couldn't go.

"You can't go either," she insisted. "Both of you. Listen. I heard my father talking to the sheriff and the rumor is that this was the work of Mike Shafer. They think he might have heard that Mr. Hess was interested in buying Trooper, so he stole him."

Everybody in Momence and thereabouts knew about the bandit Mike Shafer and his hatred for Mr. Hess. Years ago, Walter Hess had led a group of lawmen from Danville into the outlaw country of Indiana and captured Mike Shafer.

After spending a few years in prison, Shafer returned with vengeance in his heart. In the twelve years since his release, he had poisoned, butchered or stolen almost fifty head of Walter Hess's horses. Only problem with this rumor was that it was actually Jacob Hess, his son, not Walter that wanted to buy Trooper. Rumors are apt to get the details fuddled.

"We'll be careful, Libby." I wanted to put some distance between us, but she was walking along the riverbank and having no trouble keeping up.

"Mike Shafer will kill you," she assured me. "He killed his own daughter!"

I had heard this story many times. It was said that Mike Shafer had a ten-year-old daughter that talked too freely to people about the comings and goings at their place. When she told a couple of lawmen about a missing horse, Mike had had enough.

The rumor was he took her out in the marsh and cut her throat. He then pulled out some of her hair and scattered it about and claimed a wild animal carried her off.

"I heard Old Shaf was dead," Eli hollered from the back of the canoe to Libby. "We'll be fine."

We were about thirty feet from shore now, putting our backs into the paddles, but making slow progress for our effort. For every two foot we paddled forward, the current pushed us back a foot.

"You don't know he's dead!" Libby persisted.

We were in the middle of the stream now and the fog on the river had enveloped us. I could not see Libby anymore, but her insistent plea cut through the haze.

"We'll bring Scarlett back," I tried to assure her. "We'll bring your red pony back."

"I don't care. They can have Scarlett. Ben, you get back here! You're going to get yourself killed."

That was the last thing I could make out as we moved towards the opposite shore. Eli had been right. Pitting our wide, flat-bottomed rowboat against this strong spring current would be a losing battle. I pulled my Union Army Kepi hat down over my eyes and dug into the dark water with my paddle.

"Ya think she's gonna tell on us?" asked Eli.

"Naw, I swore her to secrecy," I said confidently. I didn't feel very confident though. She seemed pretty upset.

"Okay, she's yer girl so you should know her."

"She ain't my girl!" I said sharply.

"Well, she weren't hollering 'Eli, Eli. You come back here right now.'" He said this with a high, mocking voice aimed at getting me riled.

"Shut up."

Eli laughed, happy that he had amused himself at my expense, and dug his paddle deeper into the river.

~

CHAPTER 5
The Upper Crossing

After an hour of paddling, we reached the upper crossing. This ancient ford was a flat rock ledge that restricted the water of the Kankakee River and created a back-up all the way across the state line. I suppose without it, there would be no Grand Kankakee Marsh that covered hundreds of thousands of acres and extended all the way to St. Joe in Indiana.

As we approached the ford, the current got too strong and we weren't making any headway. Eli steered the canoe onto a low spot on the riverbank and we rested for a minute. He was good at steering the canoe from the stern, using a stroke with a twist at the end to keep the boat online. It looked like he was drawing the letter "J" over and over again in the water.

I sat on the bow and looked around for any sign of the first settlement in the area. Somewhere in the dangled underbrush on the far shore was the remains of William Lacy's first cabin. Thirty years ago, this point was the main ford over the Kankakee River and settlers began to build a community here. My father told me they had built a bridge over the ford to make passing easier, but the river took it out. Gradually everyone moved a mile south to our ford of the river in Momence. They built a bridge there too, and so far the river has spared it.

"Do you remember the name of the town that use to be here?" I asked, gazing across the river to the opposite bank.

"They called it Lorain on account ah that was the postmaster's wife's name."

"They had a post office here?"

"Not fer long. My grandpappy said it got moved down river to Momence. Bet ya didn't know Momence was named after my other granddaddy Mo-men-za. His daddy was a half-breed Pottawattamie chief."

I had heard this from my father, but Eli had never mentioned it before, and I had never brought it up. I had always been curious though.

"So this Mo-men-za was your grand-daddy on your momma's side?"

"Yeah. I'm ah French and Indian, Negro Englishman. A little bit of everything and not much ah anything." Eli looked kind of down in the mouth after he got all this said and we just sat quietly watching the river rush by us.

I felt bad for Eli because I have noticed that if you are part one thing and part another thing, neither one of them run up to you and give you a big hug. I don't know why that is. It doesn't make any sense to me, but that's the way it is.

After a few minutes, Eli stood up and took a length of rope and tied it to the bow. We walked the canoe the rest of the way. Above the upper crossing, the river was calmer. The water to the east spread out into broad coves and bayous. We climbed back in the canoe and began paddling, but it was difficult to make out where the channel of the river was.

After spending a lot of time paddling into a waterway that proved to be a dead end, Eli picked a yellow flower from the bank. I think it was a daisy, but I don't know much about flowers. When we got back to what we believed was the main channel, he stopped paddling and turned to me.

"Well, we made it through the rough part. Now our big problem is makin' sure we're in the main channel and not goin' up another dead-end stream."

I stared anxiously at the watery maze before us. A lot of tall reeds stretched up everywhere and it was impossible to see how far the many channels went.

"I thought you knew the way," I said. "You been here before."

"No, I ain't never been here before. I told ya I been to the big lake with my grand-pappy. I know the lake. The lake is maybe five miles south of here."

"How are we going to get this canoe five miles south to the lake?" It seemed like a fair question.

"We gonna find the ditch."

"What ditch?" Then I remembered Libby's map and pulled it out to study it. Sure enough, I found a line going from the river to the lake and it was labelled Puett's ditch. It looked to be maybe four or five miles passed the state line.

"Who is this Puett and why did he dig a ditch?"

"He dug ah ditch ta drain the lake."

"Drain the lake," I said. "This lake looks like it's huge. That would flood out Momence."

"Well, he was an Indiana guy, so he probably wasn't worried 'bout that. Didn't make no difference cause it didn't work too good. Kept pluggin' up. Just drained the lake enough ta make ah new shoreline 'round it."

"That's just plum crazy. Why would any-body want to drain Beaver Lake?"

"Make more farmland, I guess."

"Well, that's just nuts. We have plenty of farmland around here, but a nice, big lake, that's something special. Sounds like they're messing with something God put here."

"Can't grow nothing on a lake. God should know better than ta stand between a man and his profit."

"That sounds sorta like blasphemy, Eli."

"There ya go with those big words again."

A flock of red-headed teal took flight and passed about four foot over our heads. I nearly fell out of the canoe. Eli laughed at how startled I was.

"Hey, Ben, ya shoulda reached up with yer paddle and smacked one down fer din-ner."

As we got closer to the border, Eli stopped every so often and tossed a petal of the yellow flower into the water.

"If it moves downstream from us," he explained, "we are still in the channel of the river."

As the sun rose in the sky, the amount of wildlife increased. We saw a bunch of geese, wood ducks and an occasional blue

31

heron. There were deer thick as could be on a sandy island we passed. I thought of a story my father once told me of a hunter who fired at a deer while another was crossing behind it in the opposite direction and he killed both of them with one shot. Now I can't say for sure it happened, but as I watched, I thought it was possible.

When the sun was high overhead, I turned around towards Eli. "Do you think we're in Indiana yet?"

"Darned if I know."

That was not the answer I wanted to hear, but at least it was an honest one. After another mile of paddling, I heard what my tired body desired.

"Hey, Ben. Lookie that, Indiana!"

On the right side of the river in front of us appeared a sign that read: *Welcome to Indiana.* It was leaning, faded and very crudely constructed on two pieces of board and the writing was sloppy and hard to read.

It didn't look like the work of a government survey crew, but I had no reason to doubt it.

~

CHAPTER 6
Shore Lunch

After we paddled a ways into Indiana, Eli steered the boat towards shore.

"Sun's already passed high noon," he said, shielding his eyes with his arm as he looked skyward. "You ready for lunch yet?"

"Heck yes." My stomach was as empty as a bad preacher's collection plate on Sunday. Eli guided the canoe onto the shore, and I jumped out and pulled it up onto the sand with Eli still sitting in the stern.

"I guess you're hungry," he said with a laugh. "Thought this little sand dune would be ah good spot fer lunch."

"Yeah, sure is pretty here." I stood up straight and arched my back trying to get the kinks out from hours of paddling. There was no shade, but the springtime sun felt good on my skin after a long winter. Eli stepped out of the canoe with our sack of provisions. We sat on either side of the enclosed bow of the canoe, shoulder-to-shoulder, eating corn dodgers and sharing swigs of water out of the canteen.

A ruffled grouse hopped up on a log close to us and began beating his wings, making a drumming sound.

"That's ah male," said Eli. "It's matin' season and he's showing off fer the girls."

"Rusty would stop all his shenanigans real quick."

"Yeah, old Rusty would be shaggin' him outah here."

Rusty was my little beagle, a fearless bird dog, who we found dead last week. He had disappeared for several days and me and Eli started looking for him. We found him in the woods about a half mile from the stable. His belly was bloated and there were flecks of dried froth on his mouth. I thought he ate something he shouldn't have, but Eli thought he had been poisoned.

I don't believe that because Rusty was a friendly dog and everybody loved him. He was loyal and trustworthy, never straying too far from the stable. He was a great watchdog. We buried him behind the barn, and it was a sad day for me and Eli.

"So where do you think this drainage ditch is?" I wanted to change the subject before I got too melancholy thinking about poor Rusty. I had started to cry when we put Rusty in the ground and I couldn't risk that happening again. Everybody knows only lit-tle boys cry and we were on a mission for men.

"The ditch should be right around here," Eli replied. "We dun gone ah couple miles into Indiana. Should be right around here. We gotta find it. I don't hanker ta drag this canoe five miles through the brush to Beaver Lake."

I took out the hand drawn map that Libby made for me. I wish I had the original map, but she said it was pretty big. I didn't want the responsibility anyway. Maps are rare and valuable around these parts and I still had to get Libby's canoe home, not to mention her red pony. I didn't want to take the chance of losing or damaging her father's map.

Eli finished his corn dodgers and licked the crumbs off his fingers. After taking an-other swig from the canteen, he got up and walked to the crest of the low-lying dune that we were beached upon. He looked around for a moment before speaking. "This channel behind this here dune might be where da ditch empties into. When it was dug fourteen years ago, this dune might not ah even been here. Sand is always getting' blown around."

"So, ah, what do you want to do?"

"Let's split up fer a spell. You go right and I'll go left and we'll see if the ditch is emptyin' intah this back channel somewhere."

It sounded like a plan to me, so I headed up the crest of the dune going right which was back towards Illinois. The sand was getting in my shoes, so I took them off and hung them around my neck. I walked barefooted letting the soft warm sand sift between my toes. The midday sun was shining down on me and made me forget the cold winter we had just endured.

June was right around the corner and that made me feel good. School was out and I had a whole summer to look forward to. It seemed to me that a kid's life was always more interesting in the summer. I saw a black snake sunning on a flat rock on the opposite shore. He was going to like summer too.

This back channel was only about forty feet wide, and I spotted what looked like an indented place on the opposite shore that I thought might be the entrance to the ditch. It was covered in bulrushes and reeds, so it was hard to tell if it really went anywhere. To take a look, I slid down the dune and into a wet area. I was standing in about an inch of water with sand beneath it, staring at the opening across the channel. When I looked down, my feet had disappeared.

"Dang it!" I tried to lift my right foot and met with resistance. I gave it a jerk to free it, but then my left foot sank in farther. I reached down and pulled on my left leg trying to wrestle that foot out of the sand. Then it hit me like a kick in the pants.

"Quicksand!" I shouted but there was no one there to hear but a curious fox who was staring at me from the other side of the channel. As I sank in up to my knees, panic set in. The more I struggled to free myself, the deeper I sank.

"Help," I yelled hoarsely, the terror I was feeling was tightening the muscles in my throat.

"Help!" This time my plea rang loud and clear over the marsh. *Where was Eli?*

As I sank in up to my waist, I pictured myself slipping entirely below the sand, my hand stretching towards heaven as my head sunk out of sight. Never in my young life had I felt so helpless. How do you brace yourself for a slow, certain death when you are twelve years old? I hadn't begun to live.

I thought of all the things I had planned to do. I was going to go out west and be a mountain man exploring the Rockies. I wanted to become a ship captain and sail around the world. Most of all, I wanted to get Tanner Stables back to making money and being the solid business that it was when my father left for the war—the time when everything changed in my life. Libby's father had returned, and her life was more or less normal. The war was like a game of chance. It left some people's lives the same and some, it turned their lives upside down.

Libby. It occurred to me I would never see her again. She might never know what had happened to me. I took my shoes from around my neck and the army hat off my head and laid them on the wet sand. When Eli found them, he would figure out what happened to me. Maybe they could place a marker by this spot. Probably be of no use. Eli was right. The sand is always shifting.

I saw a buzzard flying overhead. *Is it going to start circling me?* My panic was moving towards outright terror. I am too young to die in this sandpit.

"Eli! Where are you? Eli!"

"Hey, young fellow, you look like you need some help there."

I turned at the waist and looked up towards the voice. He was an adult, but a very young one. He had binoculars draped around his neck and a notebook in his hand. His dress was odd for the marsh; he was wearing a suit and tie.

"Please help me if you can before I sink below the sand." My voice sounded pathetic.

He skidded down the side of the dune and, from a safe distance, put his hands on his hips and assessed my situation. "First, don't worry about slipping below the sand. In quicksand, you sink only to the point to where you displace your own bodyweight. The real problem is you will probably get a sunstroke if you are stuck there long enough without your hat."

"I was putting it over there so Eli would know where I disappeared."

"Who's Eli? Where is he?"

"He's looking for the ditch that was dug to drain Beaver Lake."

"Well, you can put your hat back on. The sand is not going to suck you completely under. Let me find a branch or something for you to hold on to so I can drag you out."

He struggled up the side of the dune and when he reached the crest, he had some advice. "You're a limber young fellow. Just flop backwards so your weight is distributed evenly, and you won't sink any more. I'll be back in a minute."

I did what he suggested and now I was alone again, staring straight up at the blue sky. The bright sun was beating down on me. I stretched over and picked up my hat to put over my face. After a while, I took it off to check for the man that was supposed to rescue me. Looking up, the buzzard was there again. *I'm sure he's circling me.*

"Ben, what the heck you doin'?"

I rolled over and saw Eli sliding down the side of the dune towards me.

"I'm bird watching! What the heck do you think I'm doing. I'm sinking in quicksand."

"Oh, I shoulda warned ya," he said. "There's a lot uh that stuff out here in the marsh."

"I'm sorry that slipped your mind. Now can you get me out of here?"

"Yeah, sure. Hold on and I'll go back to the canoe and get the rope."

"Some guy in a suit and tie went to get a branch or something. It will probably take both of you to pull me out of here."

"A guy in ah suit and tie? What ya talking about?"

Before I had to give a long explanation, the man appeared at the top of the sand dune. The suit coat was off and the tie was hanging loosely around his neck. Under his arm was one end of a large branch that he was dragging. He was sweating so I know he put a lot of effort into rescuing me.

Eli was halfway up the dune and stopped in wide-eyed amazement.

"Hey, young fella, come up here and help me with this branch."

"I was gonna go get a rope outah the canoe."

"I saw your canoe back there. This branch will do the trick. I doubt if you have enough rope to pull him out anyway."

"We got fifty feet."

The man looked surprised at this, but continued hauling the branch down to me. It was over twenty feet long and about four inches thick with a few thinner sprouts coming out the side. Eli picked up the other end and carefully moved around the water covered pit I was in.

"When we lay this on your chest," said the man, "I want you to wrap your arms around it tight."

"Yeah, pretend it's Libby," Eli chided.

I shot him a dirty look but didn't reply. I needed to save my breath. After fighting to free myself from the sand for the better part of an hour, I didn't have much left. Locking my arms around the branch, I nodded that I was ready.

"We are going to lift you up and back so there is no more downward pressure to make you sink any farther. Move your legs back and forth as much as you can. That will help free them."

Both Eli and the man were straining as they walked me backwards out of the quicksand.

When I was free up to my knees, it went faster. I kicked back and forth until my right leg was out, then I worked my left leg free from the clinging sand. They lifted the branch off my chest; I didn't have the strength to raise it. For several minutes, all I could do was gaze up at the sky. I saw the buzzard still circling above me. *Go find another meal today, you miserable scavenger.*

~

CHAPTER 7
The Primitive Cabin

I was sitting by the side of the channel putting on my shoes. The man had recovered his suit coat and was standing by me with his hands on his hips, as if he was expecting something. He was smiling, but he still made me nervous. I could sense he was full of questions.

"So where are you fellas from?"

"We come from Momence," I answered, pointing to the west.

"Now there's a coincidence. That's where I'll be going soon. My father has a farm near there. His name is Shronts," he said, extending his hand down to me. "I'm John Shronts."

"Please to meet you, sir." I got up to shake his hand.

"And what is your name, young man?" he asked. "I know this sturdy fellow must be Eli but what's your name?"

"I'm Ben."

"Ben what? You must have a last name. I know of people in Momence."

"Tanner," I said hesitantly. I couldn't think of a good reason not to tell him the truth.

"Tanner," he repeated. "There is a Tanner Livery Stable in town. Are you related to those Tanners?"

"Yeah, they are shirt-tail relatives." Eli gave me a sidelong glance but said nothing. I figured I had already given this gentleman more information than I cared too. In a way, I was glad he knew my full name because if we disappeared during this great adventure, they will know where to look for us.

"And what about you, Eli?"

"Ah, I'm Eli Brown. I'm from Hopkins Park, truth be known."

"So, what brings you fellas out here in the wilds of the marsh?"

Eli and I both looked at each other. The man in the suit was pretty young, but he was still an adult. If we told him our true intent, the first thing he would want to do would be to take us back to our parents. He would probably say things like let the authorities take care of this, but we already knew they were going to do nothing.

"We come out here ta fish," said Eli finally. He wasn't very good at lying and it came out a little weak. I could tell that John Shronts was not convinced.

"Oh, I only saw one fishing pole in your canoe," he said curiously. "What are you going to do with fifty feet of rope?"

That stumped both of us. Eli looked at me like it was my turn to make up a whopper.

"Well, sir, we thought we might need it to pull the canoe through the ditch we're looking for. We heard it is mighty low on water. We want to get our canoe to Beaver Lake." I remembered telling him earlier that Eli was looking for the ditch, so I thought I'd better tell the truth, but not necessarily the whole truth.

"Oh, the entrance to the ditch is another mile or so to the east. It's overgrown with vegetation and difficult to find. Come with me and I will show you on the way back to my cabin. You can spend the night there as my guests. It's mid-afternoon already. You don't want to try to make it to Beaver Lake at night."

"You gotta cabin out here?" asked Eli.

"Well, it's really not mine. I was on a job interview in Lake Village, and they are giving it to me free for signing on."

"Oh, a job interview," I said, touching my throat where a tie would go. "That explains the...."

"Tie?"

"Yeah, the suit and the tie."

"What kinda job do ya gotta get all dressed up fer and they give ya ah free house ta live in?" asked Eli.

"They want me to come to this area to practice medicine. I will graduate from Rush Medical College soon."

"Then you are a...."

"Yes, a doctor."

~

CHAPTER 8
On to Beaver Lake

On the way to his cabin, John Shronts pointed out the entrance to Puett's Ditch that would lead us to Beaver Lake. It would have been nearly impossible for us to find it on our own since it was overgrown with cattails and reeds. It didn't seem right to turn down his hospitality since he was so helpful. Eli pulled the canoe along the river with the fifty feet of rope. This gave some weight to my story. Can't imagine what he would say if I told him the rope was to cut up and make lead ropes for four horses we were going to take off Bogus Island. Some things are best left unsaid.

"So how old are you boys?" He turned to Eli first when he asked.

"Why, I'm sixteen," said Eli. "And Ben here is fourteen. He's small fer his age, but he's a strong little fella."

I'll tell you, I didn't like the jab he gave me, but he smoothed it over a bit by saying I was strong for my age. I think I'm a regular size for a twelve-year-old and stronger than most from pitching hay and shoveling manure in the stable.

"You fellas have a lot of supplies in that canoe. Did you plan to stay in the marsh a few days?"

"Yeah, we done it a'fore," said Eli. "Ain't no big deal to us."

I've got to say, Eli was getting better at lying. I hope he doesn't get carried away with it and trip us up. The less said the better. That always seemed like good advice to me.

"So, you fellas must have very trusting parents to let you come out here in the marsh alone. As you just found out, there are a lot of dangers out here."

"I don't have no parents," said Eli. "I live with my grandpappy, and he taught me how to get along out here."

Doctor Shronts considered this for a moment, and then turned to me.

"What about you, Ben? Are your parents okay with you coming out here with all the outlaws around?"

"I only have one parent. My father was an army captain and he died during the war."

"Oh, I'm sorry to hear that."

Before I had to lie again, Doctor Shronts's mind went elsewhere.

"There's the cabin up ahead. It has two rooms so you boys can have one to your-selves. It's a little far from town, but I told them I was married last year, and I needed a place large enough for a family. I will send for my wife when I have made the place more habitable."

When we got there, he pushed open the door and I'll have to admit, it wasn't very im-pressive. The cabin had a wood plank floor that looked like it wanted to give you splin-ters. You could still see bark on the logs in the walls. I couldn't imagine a doctor's wife wanting to live here, but they were young. When you're young and in love, nothing else matters. That's something I heard my mother say, anyhow.

Doctor Shronts put his binoculars and notebook on a crude looking table made of split logs. He took off his coat and hung it on a peg near the fireplace.

"I know it's nothing fancy, but it's better than you boys sleeping out there in the wild."

"It's fine, sir," I insisted.

"Beats sleepin' in the swamp," Eli chimed in. "Don't have ta worry about no critters sneakin' up on ya in the dark."

49

Me and Eli were sitting at the rough-hewn table while Doctor Shronts paced back and forth in front of the unlit fireplace as he spoke. "Yes, there are a lot of creatures out there. The Grand Kankakee Marsh has always had a special fascination for me ever since I was a boy. My father first brought me out here hunting when I was ten."

"This is a great place ta hunt, I know," said Eli. "My grandpappy been taking me out here since I was nine."

I don't know whether he was just stating a fact or felt he had to "one up" John Shronts. Eli did pride himself on being able to survive in the wilderness, so maybe he felt he had to be more rugged than anyone wearing a suit and tie.

"Speaking of hunting," said the doctor, "I shot a deer early this morning and dressed it out in the back. We will have venison tonight unless the coyotes got to it."

"I'm more afraid of wolves," I admitted.

"And rightly so. Wolves are bigger and more aggressive than coyotes. They hunt in packs and will attack a man if they are hungry enough. We have them both out there in the marsh. It is teeming with wildlife from huge buffalo down to little chipmunks."

"I seen buffalo a'fore," said Eli. "Down by the shore of the big lake."

"The big lake was bigger when I was here as a kid," said the doctor. "Puett's ditch drained off some of it. That's why there is a hundred yards of sandy shoreline around Beaver Lake. Now the ditch is all plugged up and it is stabilized."

"Why did they let Puett try to drain the lake?" I asked. "That just seems to be a crazy idea."

"It was all due to the Swamplands Act of 1850," said the doctor. "Congress agreed to revert all federally held swampland to the state if they agreed to drain it and turn it into productive farmland."

"Well, the lake ain't no swamp," Eli quickly pointed out.

"That's true, but it was all part of the package for the state of Indiana. Since the ditch has plugged up, it's a moot point."

I didn't know what kind of point that was, but I guess it didn't matter if the ditch didn't work.

"There is a significant difference in elevation between the lake and the river, but the town elders in Lake Village suspect that certain individuals did not want their beautiful lake to disappear. The ditch is almost five miles long, running from the river to the lake. They could post guards to keep it open during the daylight, but a lot can happen in the middle of the night."

"Well, I'm glad that crazy notion's been forgot," said Eli.

"It's not over yet, Eli. The town elders were telling me that a businessman named Lemuel Milk from Kankakee bought the lake. You can guess what he wants to do with it."

I didn't want to guess. The whole idea of draining the lake to make more farmland was a crazy notion, just like Eli said. We got farmland all over, but there won't be any more lakes. The good Lord wasn't making any new ones.

~

CHAPTER 9
By Dawn's Early Light

At around nine o'clock we turned in and, I'll have to admit, it was nice having a good roof over our heads instead of sleeping in the marsh. Eli and I had slept outdoors before, but down by the river in town. There might be an owl hooting or a squirrel scampering around at night, but that would be nothing next to night sounds in the marsh. I would have to get used to them, though, because tomorrow night we would be camping under the stars.

I had trouble sleeping as thoughts of facing armed outlaws kept racing through my mind. *What had I talked Eli into?* The idea that a couple of kids could go into an outlaw's den and steal back their horses was pretty ridiculous.

You know, if you look at it from an adult's point of view, that is. I glanced over at Eli, who was sleeping soundly. I know he had no quit in him once he started something. That's just the way he was. I would have given up on saving Tanner Stables a couple of times, but Eli wouldn't let me. He said we had to take it one day at a time and not think about messing things up. I guess that is what we were going to have to do on this mission.

At about six in the morning, a screech owl started his courting song. It was spring and he had to do what he had to do, but I was sound asleep and I didn't appreciate it. I don't know why they call them screech owls. He sounded more like a young colt whinnying. I went to the window to close it when I heard Dr. Shronts talking to someone outside.

"The younger boy is named Ben Tanner. He's related to the family that owns Tanner Stables in Momence. He claims to be fourteen, but I would say he is more like eleven or twelve."

What! Okay, I'll accept the twelve. I don't look older than my age like Eli does. A doctor probably knows stuff to look for to tell how old someone is. My voice cracking every once in a while didn't help, but eleven! Now that was a downright insult.

"What about the other kid?" asked the visitor.

"He's older. He claims to be sixteen. He's probably younger too. His name is Eli—

at least that is what he told me. He says he's from Hopkins Park."

"So ya think they're runaways, Doc?"

"I don't know if they are runaways, but they are up to something. Probably something that could get them hurt. They are too young to be running around out here in the marsh by themselves."

"Okay, when I get back to town, I will send a telegraph over to Momence ta see if they're missing."

"Good. I'll keep them here until I hear from you."

"I would guess the Justice of the Peace will want to take them into custody until the parents show up to take them home."

Oh, no! The Doc is on to us. The whole plan was falling apart in one day. Then a small voice inside me said, *this whole thing is a crazy idea. What were you thinking? You're only twelve years old!* Then someone grabbed my shoulder, and the small voice of reason was gone.

"We gotta get outah here," Eli whispered.

We had slept in our clothes so that when we got our shoes on, we'd be ready to go. All except one thing. We had brought all our food inside. It didn't seem like a good idea to leave it out at night in an open canoe for all the critters of the marsh to steal.

"You keep on listenin'," Eli said, "and I'll get our grub outah the other room."

When I heard the man on the horse ride away, I went to the door. "Eli, hurry up! He'll be coming in the house."

Eli had no sooner shut the bedroom door behind him when we heard John Shronts entering the cabin. We silently escaped out the bedroom window and were gone. The canoe was down by the river, and we slid it into the water. A morning fog hung over the marsh, so we were out of sight with a few paddle strokes.

Eli steered the canoe to the opposite bank so we could find the entrance to the ditch. The fog was good for giving us cover, but it made locating the ditch much harder. We had almost passed it when Eli saw the big oak tree that he said marked the entrance.

No water appeared to be flowing out of the ditch and the mouth was filled with cattails and reeds. Eli decided the easiest way to go forward would be to portage the canoe along the bank of the ditch. We landed beside the entrance and lifted the canoe out of the water. It was on the heavy side with all our supplies in it and I was glad the waterway was not choked with weeds after we were a hundred yards in. We were able to put the canoe in the shallow water and pulled it along with the rope. After making our way south for a mile, Eli thought it was safe to stop and rest. Exhausted, we both dropped to the ground. The canoe was floating in several inches of stagnant water.

"You suppose we're going to get to a place deep enough we can get in and paddle to the lake?" I asked.

"Don't look like it. Looks pretty choked up as far as I can see."

I looked down at the man-made waterway that was covered in green scum and lily pads. The water flow from the lake was hardly more than a trickle.

"Didn't the doctor say the elevation of the lake was considerable higher than the river?"

"Yeah, believe he did say that," replied Eli. "And why ya keep callin' him ah doctor. He ain't graduated yet and he don't have nothin' official ta hang on the wall."

"Well, he's already practicing medicine. He said he delivered a baby yesterday. Isn't that what a doctor does?"

Eli paused as he considered this. "Yeah, I suppose doin' the job makes ya a doctor more than a piece of paper."

This came as a surprise. I had actually said something and Eli agreed with me.

"Well, enough of this here lollygaggin'," said Eli. "We gotta get going if'un were gonna get ta the lake today."

We both grabbed ahold of the rope and tugged the canoe full of our gear and grub through the shallow water for another mile. At several points we had to get down in the water because there were so many reeds and cattails on the bank we could not pass. After another hour or so, we collapsed on the bank of the ditch. The sun had risen in the sky, and we were both sweating.

"We need a couple uh them machetes," said Eli.

"What's that?"

"It's a big knife they use to cut through stuff like this. My grandpappy had one that he got from his daddy. He come from one ah those islands where they use ah machete to chop sugar cane."

"You mean in the Caribbean Sea?"

"Yeah, I guess. If that's where Jamaica be."

"You sure got an interesting family tree, Eli."

"Yeah, they brung in parts from all over ta make me."

I looked along the ditch and wondered how close we were to the lake. I would guess that we were about halfway. We were hoping to reach it before noon, but it was slow going so far. As I looked south, I saw something moving about a quarter of a mile ahead. I thought at first it was a deer, but then it stood up.

"Is that a man up ahead?"

"What?" Eli had been sitting hunched over watching the sweat drip off his nose.

He stood up, leaned forward and squinted in the direction I was pointing.

"Believe it is," he said. "Let's get this canoe moving and maybe we can catch up with him."

We crawled back into the ditch and Eli took the lead on the rope. We gave it our all. When we were half the distance to the man, he disappeared. Our pace slowed down after that. We lost our need to hurry.

"Guess that fella weren't in no mood ta talk."

"Guess not," I replied, being too short of breath for any lengthy conversation. Then, as I'm apt to do, my brain started imagining things. "Maybe he was an outlaw. That's why he scurried off."

"Maybe."

"You suppose we spooked him?"

"Sure. He's a big, bad outlaw and two kids pullin' ah canoe spooked him," said Eli. "And one looks like he's only eleven."

"Dang. You heard that?" The only reply from Eli was a snicker of a laugh.

~

CHAPTER 10
A Dweller of the Swamp

When we got to the place where the man had disappeared, we found a dam built across the ditch. Part of it looked like the work of beavers, but the newest repair was the work of man. There was a woven fence across the top of the dam where it had been leaking and rock and dirt piled against it to hold back the water. We were relieved to see that there was enough water built up behind the dam to float the canoe with us in it.

After we carried the canoe over the dam, Eli took his place in the rear and had me sit in the front. It felt good to be afloat again. He jammed his paddle into the water and half of it disappeared before he struck bottom.

"Plenty deep 'nough here."

"We still won't have to worry about drowning if we tip over."

Eli pushed us off and we glided south across the stagnant water. I noticed a rustling of the reeds to our right and turned to Eli to see if he heard it too.

"Yeah, I heard it. Maybe it be ah mountain lion tracking us thinkin' you were about the right size for his lunch."

"There aren't any mountain lions around here."

"How ya know that?" he said. "All kinda critters out here in the marsh."

This kicked in my overactive imagination and I was looking warily from side-to-side. I didn't notice we had a more immediate and real problem until Eli pointed it out.

"We got a leak."

I turned from my seat in the bow and saw an inch of water sitting in the middle of the canoe, the lowest point.

"What caused that?"

"Draggin' it 'bout two miles is what, I'd guess."

We landed the canoe and flipped it over; there was a patch in the middle that had been ripped loose. Libby had not mentioned it had a weak spot. The canoe had been a birthday gift from her grandfather and was constructed of varnished canvas stretched over a wood frame. We did pull it over a lot of branches and rocks, so I guess some damage could be expected.

"What are we going to do now, Eli?"

"Don't rightly know."

"We can't get to Bogus Island without a boat."

He looked at the ripped canvas patch and I didn't see his face light up like he had some great idea. Then Eli looked passed me with a concerned look. I turned to see what he was looking at.

"**Aaaah!**"

I came face-to-face with a strange swamp creature, half man and half beast. I jumped over the canoe and rolled down the bank, almost ending up in the stagnant water of the ditch. I thought Eli would be right behind me, but when I looked up, he had stood his ground and was standing face-to-face with the creature.

As I stared at it, I gradually realized that what I had thought was a strange swamp-creature was actually an old Indian with a wolf's pelt over his head and shoulders. He stared at Eli unsmiling, but not unfriendly. His skin was dark and wrinkled.

Raising both hands, palms out, he said, "Kwe Kwe."

"Ni je wa," Eli responded in kind.

I didn't know what all that meant but it sounded friendly enough and I crawled back up the bank of the ditch.

The old Indian eyed Eli curiously.

"Are you tribal?" he asked.

"My grandmother was Pottawatomi."

"Hmm." The old Indian considered this for a moment as he looked down at Eli's moccasins. He nodded his head in approval.

"I am Gray Wolf. Last of Shawnee. All others leave." He made a sweeping gesture with his hand to the west when he said this.

"What happened to the rest?" I blurted out, then wished I hadn't. I knew the native people were pushed out of the area before I was born. It was probably something the old man did not want to talk about. Eli gave me a look like I was a ninny.

"All driven out after war. Tecumseh killed and Shawnee pushed out. The Prophet was no leader. He tell us before battle for Prophetstown his magic would turn away the white soldier's bullets." He pointed to a scar at the side of his head. "I was young warrior. I believed him."

"You were shot in the side of your head?" I asked.

"It knock me out. I laid there and wolves come to feed on bodies. This one," he pointed to the wolf pelt on his head and shoulders, "he want to eat me. I kill him."

"So that's where you get your name, Gray Wolf?"

The old warrior nodded his head to tell me this was true. I looked at Eli and he just rolled his eyes. I guess it was pretty obvious.

The old man was standing there making a humming noise, maybe thinking of the distant past and the battles of his youth. He had to be talking about the Battle of Tippecanoe. It was fought about fifty miles south of here where the Tippecanoe River meets the Wabash.

I didn't remember the date from my brief history class with Mr. Trowbridge, but it was a cause of the War of 1812. I did the math in my head and the old Indian had to be around seventy years old.

The old warrior stopped humming and came back to the present. He walked forward and stooped over the canoe.

"Need pine tar."

"Yeah," Eli agreed. "Do you have any?"

"Not here."

Well, I guess it was no surprise he wasn't carrying around a bucket of pine tar, but it sounded promising that he had a supply somewhere. It really felt good that he wanted to help. He ran his weathered fingers over the varnish covered canvass. There was black tar residue around the six-inch slit that told me it had been patched before and we tore it off.

"Pick up," the old one said, motioning for us to lift our canoe. "Take to my camp."

I looked at Eli and he shrugged, so I picked up the bow and he grabbed the stern. We followed behind not knowing how far we had to cart the canoe. I did know we could not get to Bogus Island in a leaky boat and the old man was willing to help.

After we walked about fifty yards, we came to a clearing with a crude hut in the middle. It looked like it began as a lean-to and that a front and sides were added later. The old man pointed to a stump, and I hoisted the damaged end onto it. A rabbit was roasting on a spit over an open fire. Eli and I must have both been eyeing it.

"You eat. Young warriors need food to be strong."

He didn't have to tell us a second time. We had not stayed around for breakfast at Dr. Shronts's place and were as hungry as a short-armed man at a boarding house breakfast.

"How long ya think it'd be ta fix?" Eli asked between bites. Juice was running down his chin.

"Need canvass to fix good. Must go to town."

"Can't you just put a big gob of pine tar on it?" I asked. "There's some bad guys stole four of our horses. It happened four days ago. If we don't get to Bogus Island soon, they will have shipped those horses out to who knows where."

The old warrior considered this a moment before he replied. "You take my canoe." He pointed to a birch bark Indian canoe next to his lean-to. It had a high prowl in front that curved backwards and almost pointed to the occupants.

"We couldn't do that," Eli protested before I could give him a kick in the shin.

"We'll take good care of it, sir," I put in quickly.

The old man shook his head and moved toward the canoe. I turned to Eli and gave him a thumbs up. When we picked it up, we discovered it was heavier than Libby's canvass canoe. Our effort brought the first smile to the old man's face. He stepped faster and caught up with me, grabbing the rear of the birch bark canoe.

"Small warrior need some help."

Eli turned and gave me a mischievous smile. When we got to the bank of the ditch, we set down the canoe and sat down to rest for a minute. The old warrior stood over us with a concerned look on his face.

"I will go with. Show where trail under water is. You lead horses out. I bring canoe back."

He said this in a way that told us there was not going to be any discussion about it. I guess he wanted to make sure he got his canoe back. Could not blame him for that. A couple of kids going up against hardened outlaws would not seem like a good bet in anybody's book. *But what was this hidden trail he mentioned?*

"Gray Wolf," Eli said. "What's this trail under da water you're talkin' about?"

"I will show you." He said this as he slid the canoe down the bank and into the ditch. Me and Eli looked at each other with raised eyebrows before sliding down to the waiting canoe. Gray Wolf motioned with his hand for us to wait and headed back towards his camp.

We busied ourselves swatting sandflies and catching our breath until he returned. He reappeared shortly with a bow, three arrows wrapped in dry grass, and a bottle of clear liquid. He sat down in the middle of the large canoe and arranged these mysterious items around him.

"Moon tonight," he said as if that was an explanation.

Eli and I looked at each other and shrugged our shoulders. We spent last night under a roof and hadn't noticed the phases of the moon.

"We go."

At this command, Eli and I dipped our paddles into the stagnant water and we were off.

~

D. N. Bedeker

CHAPTER 11
On Beaver Lake

The birch bark canoe had a deeper draft than Libby's canvass covered one and Eli and I had to jump out after we had gone a mile and pull it over a low spot in the ditch. Gray Wolf did not get out but waited patiently for us to push him into deeper water. After we struggled for another mile, I looked up and saw no trees ahead of us. The lake must be near.

The ditch became deeper and wider when I finally saw it—Beaver Lake. I could see why some people just called it the big lake. Looking south, it was so big that it disappeared out of sight. I could not see the opposite shore. My best estimate from using the scale on the map Libby made me was that it was about six miles going north and south, and about eight miles wide. Now, of course, the real big lake is Lake Michigan. Comparing Beaver Lake to it was like comparing a cup of water to a bathtub. But I have never seen Lake Michigan, so I was very impressed with Beaver Lake.

We got out of the canoe to stretch and look around. I offered Gray Wolf my hand since he was having some trouble getting out of the canoe. He waved it off, looking offended. I looked at Eli and he did his eye roll again. I guess extending a helping hand was not something you offered a warrior no matter how old he is. The old man struggled to stand straight after he managed to climb out. We walked the beach for about twenty yards and gradually he was standing tall, proud and upright.

The wide shore was sandy and almost bare of vegetation. Gray Wolf explained this was because years ago when Puett dug his ditch, the water did recede about a hundred yards all around the lake. I remember Doctor Shronts mentioning this too and I thought I would ask the obvious question.

"The doctor we stayed with last night said the lake was higher than the river. Why didn't Puett's ditch work and drain the whole lake?"

Gray Wolf smiled. "Damn Beavers," was all he said.

Eli pushed my shoulder and I almost fell down.

"I swear, Ben, fer a guy that's so smart he talks like ah book, you're a little slow on the uptake sometimes."

Before I could regain my balance, the pieces fell into place. When we first saw Gray Wolf, he was at the dam that held the water back and forced us to drag the canoe through stagnant water for over a mile. I'll admit, I never have seen a beaver dam, but what we ran into looked like it was constructed by man. Since there was fresh dirt on top, I guess a feller should have figured out it was the work of Gray Wolf. He was the savior of the lake.

"How long ya lived out here in the marsh?" asked Eli.

"Since white soldiers drove us out of Prophetstown. Long time."

Yes, that was a long time. Over fifty years in fact. He must have been around Eli's age when he first came to the marsh to hide. All the other members of Tecumseh's rebellious tribe had been chased west. Gray Wolf, survivor of the Battle of Tippecanoe, was the last Shawnee.

Standing tall, Gray Wolf pointed to a dark smudge on the horizon to the southeast.

"Island of the horse thieves," he announced.

I took my father's binoculars out of the bow and focused on the island. Through the binoculars, I could see there were actually two islands. The closest one was small and flat, almost like a steppingstone to the larger Bogus Island which had a giant sand dune rising to a peak in the middle. Gray Wolf was curious about something and stood by me as I gazed out upon the lake.

"Those make things close up." He said it like a statement rather than a question, so he knew what they were, but maybe had never looked through a pair. I focused them as sharp as I could and handed them to the old warrior. He looked through them and drew back, startled. Then he smiled and put them up to his eyes again.

When Gray Wolf had satisfied his curiosity, he put the binoculars back in the boat and motioned for us to get in. As we paddled, a dark cloud appeared on the horizon. It was skimming the surface of the lake. At the speed it was approaching us, I knew it was not really a cloud. As the dark mass came closer, it was only about five feet off the water and made the sound of a million wings beating in unison. Gray Wolf muttered something in Shawnee and hunched over in the canoe, yanking his wolf pelt over his head.

"It's passenger pigeons," shouted Eli.

The flock rose a few feet as it reached us and passed over our heads. The birds were flying at a high rate of speed, only about a foot apart. Some wonder of nature allowed them to do this without running into each other.

The dense formation blocked out the sun and we were in darkness for several minutes as the huge gathering passed over us. It seemed like it was a mile long. I really don't have a good idea of what a million is, but that would be my guess.

When they had passed, Gray Wolf pulled the pelt off his head and put it over the side, dragging it in the water alongside the canoe. I watched and then looked at Eli. I started laughing.

"Hey, Eli, you have bird crap in your hair."

He reached up and touched his hair, then pulled his hand away. "Ugh."

Then it occurred to me to do the same. "Ick."

We both leaned over the canoe to splash water on our heads. Unfortunately, we chose the same side. Gray Wolf had to throw his weight the other way to keep us from tipping over. The old warrior was laughing now as Eli and I splashed water on our shirts to clean them off. It was one of those things that we would laugh about someday in the future, but not right now.

As we paddled south, Gray Wolf motioned for us to stay close to the shore. I don't know why we didn't just paddle towards Bogus island. Hugging the shore was going to add some distance to the trip.

"Why don't we just go straight across?" I blurted out.

"Must wait for dark," he replied. "Outlaws watching."

"Yeah, Ben, they're probably up on the high ridge looking around with a spyglass."

I felt foolish for having asked my question. Sometimes my mouth gets ahead of my brain. Since we had some time to spare, we rested for a while before paddling to the shore. We landed just as the sun disappeared below the horizon. Gray Wolf got out of the canoe and walked along the edge of the water holding one of the paddles. At one point he entered the water and poked around with the paddle until he hit something solid. The old man turned to us and smiled, motioning with his hand for us to join him in the water. He then turned and began walking straight for the island. When he was about thirty yards out, the water was still only up to his knees.

"What da ya make of that?" Eli whispered.

"This must be a very shallow lake."

We walked directly towards him, but did not enter the water at the same spot he did. After Eli and I ventured out about twenty feet, there was a drop off and we were in over our heads. We flailed our way towards him, coughing and spitting up water. Gray Wolf got a laugh out of that. When we reached him, we bumped into the ends of logs that had been buried under the water.

We climbed up on them, and to our surprise, we were standing on an underwater bridge made of logs stacked in a corduroy fashion. Gray Wolf pointed to the high sandy peak on Bogus island and told us there was a sand bar that ran towards where we were standing. It ended about a hundred yards offshore, so the outlaws built a submerged bridge out of logs to get out to it.

Pretty clever if you think about it. They could ride on horseback out to Bogus Island with the horses they had stolen in tow. A posse might track them to the edge of the lake and wonder how they disappeared. Not knowing of the bridge, there wouldn't be too many members of the posse who would want to swim with their horse almost two miles to get to the island. That would not be a way to keep your gunpowder dry.

Eli walked over to me after conferring with Gray Wolf.

"Here's the plan," he announced. "We're gonna go out there in the canoe so Gray Wolf don't have ta walk two miles in the water. We'll foller the sandbar so we know where it is when we're comin' back with the hosses."

"Why doesn't Gray Wolf just leave in the canoe from here? We can walk out to the island."

"Oh, he wants ta go along. He's got a little surprised up his sleeve."

Before I could ask what it was, Eli turned and walked away. He enjoyed keeping me in the dark sometimes. I guess it made him feel like the adult.

Our plan was to wait until after dark and canoe out to the smaller island which some called "Little Bogus Island". It was formed when the sand bar that extended all the way to Bogus Island rose barely out of the water for a few hundred yards. Here we would give Gray Wolf his canoe back and Eli and I would rest and dry our clothes. We were lucky it was such a warm day for May. Later in the night, we would walk on the sandbar onto Bogus Island. We would locate our horses, if they were still there, and lead them to shore on the secret outlaw passageway through the water.

"The plan sounds easy enough," I said to Eli.

"Hmm," was his only reply.

Eli started cutting up the fifty feet of rope I brought and making halters for the horses. As we waited for the afterglow of sunset to disappear, I saw another problem. It was a three/quarter or waxing moon last night. That meant a full moon was next in the cycle. I could see it rising behind Bogus Island to the east. When we got close to our destination, we could be spotted by the outlaws in the bright moonlight.

At around eight o'clock, Gray Wolf made an announcement.

"We go now."

I like Gray Wolf because he gets to the point, and you never had to worry about him talking your ear off. Besides that, what other adult would help us do something this crazy?

You have to figure though, he was a warrior who was wounded in battle and fought a wolf to survive when he was Eli's age. I guess in the white man's world where I was growing up, kids were seen as helpless a lot longer. In Gray Wolf's world, you either grew up fast or you didn't grow up at all.

We found that following the underwater trail was not that easy. The sun had set and the rising moon was our only light. Gray Wolf directed us as we moved the canoe back and forth, poking into the water to make sure we were over the sandbar. In some places the water was deeper, but never more than two feet.

~

CHAPTER 12
The Outlaw Islands

As we came closer to the first island, the sand bar became wider and the water shallower. The "hogback," that's what the old timers would call it, came out of the water for a ways and produced the smaller island that was long and narrow and only a couple acres. It was a stopping off point to Bogus Island which was much larger, maybe forty or fifty acres by my guess.

The worry I had was the moonlight. They would probably have a lookout posted at the top of that high sand hill. The light of the full moon would give him a good view of us as we crossed the stretch of water between the two islands.

We skirted around the smaller island, keeping close to the shore for cover. There were a lot of cherry trees making a home there and Eli said his people called it "Cherry Island" instead of "Little Bogus Island." When we got to the far end of this island, we were a quarter of a mile away from Bogus Island. Gray Wolf motioned for us to get out of the canoe, and we stood on a narrow, sandy beach.

"Stay here 'til you see fire in the sky," he instructed us.

Now the thatch-wrapped arrows made sense and the bottle with the clear liquid had to be kerosene or whale oil. This was the surprise Eli had mentioned.

"We'll wait for your signal," Eli assured him.

"When you have horses, return to my camp," he said as he paddled off to the west. "I will have canoe fixed."

As he disappeared from sight, Eli turned to me, now feeling he needed to explain things to me. "He's gonna shoot those flaming arrows up in the sky to the west and get the outlaws lookin' the other way while we hightail it across to Bogus Island in the moonlight."

"I know exactly what he is doing," I said sharply. "It's a diversionary tactic."

"A what?"

"A diversionary tactic. My father told me about getting the enemy to look at one thing while you were busy doing something else."

"You sure know some big words, Ben."

"It's just like when General Lee tricked 'Fighting Joe' Hooker at Chancellorsville. He had only half as many troops as General Hooker, but he made it seem like he had more."

"That somethin' yer Daddy told you 'bout?"

"Darn straight it is."

"Why didn't he tell you about some tricky Union general?"

"Guess there weren't any. I don't know. He said the South had the best generals and that was the only thing they had going for them."

"Hmm."

"Robert E. Lee was offered the command of the Union Army, but said he could not fight against his own folks in Virginia."

"So, If'un he fought fer the North, the war woulda been a lot shorter and lots fewer fellers would be dead?"

I hesitated a moment, thinking over Eli's reasoning. "Yeah, I guess that would be so." I thought of my father who died in the spring of 1864, a year before the war ended. *Would he still be alive today?* I hated the war and now I hated Robert E. Lee.

Eli shook my shoulder, bringing me out of my somber thoughts.

"Ben, look over west."

Streaking through the sky was a flaming arrow that would certainly grab the attention of any lookout posted on the high sandhill a quarter of a mile away.

"Let's go!" I said. With lengths of rope in each hand, we frantically sloshed through the knee-deep water. We had to get to the shore and hide before Gray Wolf's distraction was over and he only had three arrows. When we got closer, the water was barely passed our ankles and we could run full speed. When we were thirty yards from the shore, a shot rang out, then another. I dove headfirst into the water.

"What are ya doin'?" rasped Eli, trying not to yell as I looked up.

"They're shooting at us."

"Do ya see any bullets splashing around us? They're shooting at Gray Wolf."

"Oh." I jumped to my feet and we ran until we hit the sandy beach and kept going until we found a bush to hide behind.

"We made it," whispered Eli.

"Yeah, don't think anybody saw us. I hope they didn't hit Gray Wolf."

"He's ah pretty cagey old guy. Bet he paddled outah range real quick."

As we huddled behind the bush, catching our breath, I had a moment of serious regret. Back in my room in Momence, this seemed like a reasonable plan. Just get out to Bogus Island, take the horses back under the cover of darkness. With the full moon, we didn't even have that. Now outlaws were shooting at a kind old man who agreed to help us. I was now fully aware that these dangerous men were a little gun happy and would not hesitate to kill us.

So far, my idea had succeeded in putting Gray Wolf and Eli in harm's way. I had an impulse to tell Eli that we should forget the whole thing. My clothes were still wet, and I shivered as the temperature dropped on this May evening. I wanted to tell Eli that we should just go home, but I knew what his response would be: *We're here now and there's no turning back.*

As we caught our breath, I tried to be satisfied that we had carried out this part of the plan. We were actually on Bogus Island. The next step would be scarier. We had to find the horses without getting ourselves killed or caught by the outlaws.

"Let's find where they got them hosses hid," said Eli. "If'un they're still here."

We entered a valley between two large sand ridges. Behind the ridge that rose up the highest, we heard voices above us. Apparently Gray Wolf's fire arrows had drawn others to the summit to figure out what was going on. They must have seen something in the moonlight. That would explain the two shots. Hopefully the ruse had worked, and Gray Wolf had gotten away unharmed. And, of course, no one had spotted us splashing ashore.

There was a cave hollowed out beneath the high sand ridge. This must be the horse thieves cave that Gray Wolf had warned us about. Half walking and half crawling, we got close enough to see an unattended fire at the entrance. Although no one was in sight, someone could be down from the summit of the ridge at any moment, so we had to look around fast. Bogus Island got its name from counterfeiters that printed bogus currency in the cave back before the Civil War.

We checked out the cave and it was their living quarters. There were makeshift beds all around and clothes hanging. I was wondering how you would dig a cave into a sandhill; there were timbers that shored up the ceiling and walls. I guess desperate men could do anything if they put their minds to it. The underwater bridge being the best example.

Eli and I cut our inspection of the cave short when we heard a horse nicker to our left. We had a direction to go on now and we moved towards the sound of the horse. A short ways from the cave, we spotted the horse corral that was tucked behind a sand dune for protection. We ran to the edge of the pen and peeked in. Libby's red pony Scarlett was close to us, right by the fence.

Then we spotted Mr. Tyler's dappled gray filly. I was glad to see her because I didn't want anything to do with a lawsuit. I really wanted to get that filly back home. I didn't see Maggie, our little sorrel mare. She was twenty years old, but still had plenty of life left in her. I really wanted to find her because, Trooper tended to follow her around. Then I saw her at the far end of the corral. She was standing there alone. *Where was Trooper?*

"I see the mare but no Trooper," said Eli, concerned, as if reading my thoughts. As my father would have put it, recovering Trooper was the primary objective of our mission. Without saying it, we both understood that.

"I hope they haven't sold him already," was my sad reply. "Maybe we're too late."

I was happy to see Libby's pony and the other horses in the corral, but Trooper was gone. The whole trip was beginning to feel like a foolish failure at this point. This was no time to get down in the dumps though.

"He may be somewhere else on the island," I said, trying to remain hopeful. "It's pretty big. Looks to be a quarter mile long. They could have put him someplace else."

"Could be," Eli admitted with a shrug. "We can't take Libby's pony, the mare and Mr. Tyler's hoss out ah the corral 'til later when we know them varmits are asleep. We miz well check the island out."

Eli's hand suddenly flew up commanding silence. Two outlaws had come down from the lookout roost to sit by the campfire. One was a big guy with a slouch hat like confederate rebels wore, the other a smaller man that walked with a limp. We both jumped behind the nearest bush.

"So what the heck was that?" asked the gimpy one, "Flaming arrows shooting across the sky." He had a definite southern accent.

"Remember Mike Shafer tellin' us about an old Indian that kept blocking up that drainage ditch they built."

"If thet were him, I'm purty sure I shot thet crazy old fool."

"Skeeter, you better hope ya didn't. Shafer don't want this lake drained so he might not look kindly on you shootin' that old Indian. You don't cross Old Shaf. Not if ya like livin' a long life."

"Well, the Sarge ain't afraid of Mike Shafer. I'll tell ya that."

"Well, the Sarge ain't here. He's nice and comfy right now sleeping in a good bed. We're here and we is the ones gotta deal with Shafer."

"Bill, I don't begrudge the Sarge ah warm bed," said Skeeter as he stirred the fire with a stick. "He done a lot fer us durin' the war. Ya know he's the best man ta be in town scoutin' fer likely horses. The Sarge knows how ta hornswoggle these Yankees. He found thet big black stallion, didn't he? The Major says thet one'll fetch a pretty penny."

"Yeah, if we ever get it back from Shafer. When's he supposed to have it done? We had to take it all the way up to his 'studio.' Makes him sound like some kinda artist or somethin'."

"Bill, the way I heard tell, he is an artist. He can change the markin's on ah horse soz nobody can tell. He said he was gonna strap ah boiled tater on the forehead of thet black stallion and when he takes it off, all the hair will fall out and white hair will grow in thet spot. He's gotta whole bunch of tricks like thet. Been doin' it fer years, way I hear it."

"If we have to wait for the hair to grow back in, that could be days. The Major will be back tomorrow or the next day. Skeeter, you can tell him we ain't got the stallion."

"Why me?"

"Yer the one dun sided with Sarge when he come up with the idea of getting' this Mike Shafer in the deal. I says let's take our chances nobody will identify the black horse."

"Sarge said the best market fer thet stallion was Chicago," said Skeeter. "We can't sell it thet close without changin' some marking."

"The Major decides where the horses get sold, not the Sarge. And the Major don't like nobody knowin' our business. He's liable ta order us ta kill this Mike Shafer."

This caused a moment of silence. The two outlaws just looked at each other for a while as this prospect sunk in.

"Well, if'un thet happens," said Skeeter, "Sarge would come out and help us."

"Ya think so, do ya?"

Eli and I had pushed forward as close as we could to eavesdrop on these two interesting fellows. As I leaned forward, a branch cracked under my foot.

"What's that?" asked Skeeter.

They both looked towards the bushes we were hiding behind. Skeeter started to get up, but Bill motioned for him to sit down. "Seems every night you hear somethin' and go trapsin' about in the dark. Relax. Probably just a squirrel crackin' a nut."

Skeeter did as he was told, but he still stared towards the bushes. Slowly, very slowly, we backed away from the two at the campfire. When we had enough forest between us and them and we could no longer see the glow of their fire, we sat down and I let out the breath I had been holding for several minutes.

"So now we know fer sure," said Eli. "Trooper ain't here. Old Shaf's got 'em."

"Yeah. I wonder where this so called 'studio' is. I'll tell you sure, Trooper's not gonna put up with somebody strapping a scalding hot potato to his forehead."

"Well, right now what we gotta worry 'bout is getting' Libby's pony, Mr. Tyler's filly and the mare outah here. Then we can worry 'bout Trooper."

CHAPTER 13
What to Do?

Well, me and Eli had a disagreement as to what to do next. He wanted to snatch Libby's pony, Maggie and Mr. Tyler's filly and skee-daddle. He felt we would have to worry about getting Trooper back later. It went along with his "bird in the hand" way of thinking. Eli's got a stubborn practical streak. For me, it was more complicated. To my way of thinking, that was taking too big of a chance we would never lay eyes on Trooper again.

"If we go back with the horses we got," I protested, "it will take us two days to get back to town. The way they were talking, this Major might be here tomorrow. He might go over to Mike Shafer's studio and get Trooper and take off."

"If Old Shaf started workin' on Trooper already, don't reckon he'll be given him up less'en he gets paid fer the job."

"The Mysterious Major or, was he Blue or was he Gray?" I muttered, half to myself.

"What?"

"The Beadle dime novel from the War Library collection. The ones that were stories about Union troops. My dad brought a bunch for me to read when he came home on leave that one time. He said the soldiers read them in camp to pass the time."

"I don't remember that one," said Eli, "but this here major is definitely gray."

We worked our way to the middle of the island and found a big flat rock to lie on. I could see the full moon peeking through the oak trees. It was very peaceful and gave me time to consider our situation.

"What was I thinking?" I asked in a sudden moment of realization. "If we take the three horses we got back to Momence, we'll have a whole bunch of adults making sure we don't leave again."

"Ain't nobody gonna be stoppin' me, but I keep forgetin' you're justa kid."

Now that was an unfair shot. I let the comment pass though, because I could use it in my favor.

"Yeah, you're right. I'm just a kid. They won't let me out of their sight and you can't do it all alone. That's the reason we got to stay here and bring all the horses home together."

Eli sat there a moment not saying a word, just thinking. Then he smiled and I knew he had come up with some kind of plan.

"We'll leave these horses with Gray Wolf," he said. "Then we can come back and watch fer'em ta bring Trooper back."

"What if they shot Gray Wolf? We don't know."

"The little nervous guy with the limp did all the shootin'. You heard them. I don't think he could be much of ah deadeye shooter. Probably couldn't hit the broad side of a barn."

"Yeah, you're right. He is really twitchy."

"Okay then, we need ta wait here 'til those varmits are asleep. Sun went down about two hours ago so it must be 'round ten o'clock."

I laid back on the big rock and stared up at the open sky.

"If we wait until the moon gets behind that last oak tree over there," said Eli, "should be after midnight."

"Fair enough. That's when we'll make our move."

With that decided, all there was to do was wait. I twisted around trying to find a comfortable spot on the rock, but I didn't want to get too comfortable and fall asleep. Eli was never much for small talk, but I was going to give it a try.

"How many stars do you think are up there?" I asked since we were both gazing at the cloudless night sky.

"Don't rightly know. I can see a couple dozen, maybe more."

"King George's Royal Astronomer thought there might be millions."

"Who's this guy?"

"Sir William Herschell was his name. Mr. Trowbridge met him once when he lived in England. He told us all about him. Herschell started out supporting himself as a musician but as his reputation in astronomy spread, King George made him his Royal Astronomer."

"So he got paid just to look up at the stars?"

"Well, yes, but there was more to it than that."

"Hmm."

A herd of deer walked into the clearing in front of us and interrupted my thoughts of the far away stars. There were three does and four newborn fawns rummaging for food in the moonlight. There was one doe that looked like she was in charge. She kept looking around warily and when she spotted us lying on the flat rock, she gave out a grunt and they all scattered.

"How do you think they got out here on this island?" I asked.

"Probably just born here. Could have swum out."

"Deer can swim?"

"Dang straight. Deers are good swimmers."

Or maybe they saw the horses travelling the underwater road. I didn't say this to Eli because I already looked pretty clueless about deer. I wondered if deer could figure out how to use the underwater bridge. Everybody seems to think animals are really dumb, but sometimes I doubt that. My father used to say raccoons were so smart, if you give them some time, they could figure out how to hitch up a horse and steal your wagon.

"Okay, Ben, I think we waited longa 'nough. Them varmits should be asleep by now."

My stomach clinched as I thought of creeping into the corral and taking our horses back. It didn't seem like such a perilous undertaking two nights ago, safe and secure in my bedroom. My mind would often fill with dangerous adventures before I drifted off to sleep. I was always amazingly brave in all these imaginary undertakings. Now the danger was real, and I was not feeling brave at all. I was thinking of two armed outlaws and all the things that could go wrong.

The trail back to the corral was well lit by the moon and that was both a blessing and a curse. If the outlaws woke up, we would be good targets in the moonlight. Eli had assured me the outlaws would not take turns keeping guard all night since they felt very secure on the island. Why would they think anyone would be crazy enough to come out to Bogus Island, a known outlaw hideout, and try to reclaim the horses in the middle of the night? But here we were. At least we had surprise on our side.

Eli raised his hand to signal a stop as we left the protective darkness of the trees. I felt so exposed in the moonlight and my heart sped up a few beats. We crept very cautiously towards the gate of the corral. Eli knelt down and began opening the loops on two lassos. He gave a third one to me.

"I'll lead Maggie and Mr. Tyler's filly out," he whispered. "You get Libby's pony.

She knows you better than me. Them Shetland can be ornery."

Eli crouched down and stealthily moved forward. I did the same, but when we got close to the corral, I started crawling on my hands and knees. When we were a few feet away, one of the horses snorted and I flattened on the ground behind a small bush.

Then I heard a noise—a rattling sound a few feet in front of me. I froze when the serpent's head rose up in the grass.

~

CHAPTER 14
Into the Darkness

I thought my heart had stopped. I really did. A few feet in front of me a rattlesnake was readying itself to strike, it's serpentine body slithering into a coiled position, its vibrating rattle announcing my impending death. The viper's head drew back, and its split tongue flicked menacingly towards my face. I was paralyzed with fear. I could not move.

"**Urgh**," I grunted after rudely being jerked backwards, my face bouncing on the grass. Eli had grabbed me by the ankles and pulled me back from danger. The snake did not strike, but slithered into the darkness.

"Oh my—" I got out before Eli put his hand over my mouth.

"Sssh," he warned before removing his hand. I started shaking and he pulled me backwards away from the corral. We retreated another fifty feet behind a fallen tree.

"Oh my God, I could have been killed," I gasped as quietly as I could. "I didn't know snakes came out at night."

"What'd ya think they did?"

"I don't know. I guess they just crawled into their snake holes and went to sleep."

In spite of the danger we were in, Eli had to chuckle at that. "Now I suppose ya gonna ask me how he got out here on this island."

"Let me guess. Rattlesnakes can swim too."

"That's right."

"What if he had struck and bit me after you pulled me back."

"Oh, you was alright. They know how far they can strike and it's only 'bout half ah their length. He weren't a big one. Ya most likely scared him as much as he scared you."

"Well, I'm glad you weren't worried."

Eli motioned me to be quiet as he crouched down further behind the log. Skeeter had come out of the outlaw's cave and was cautiously approaching the corral with his gun drawn. He was turning his head nervously from side to side; he had heard something. He walked the perimeter on the corral and then moved out farther. He passed by the spot where I had been lying a few minutes ago,

"Maybe the snake will bite him," I whispered.

"Sssh," was Eli's only reply.

We were relieved when Skeeter began walking away from us, leaning forward, staring into the darkness as he went.

"Skeeter, what the hell ya doin' out there?" came an angry voice from inside the outlaw cave.

"Thought I heard something."

"Only thing ya heard was critters roamin' around in the night. Get in here fer some big horned owl picks up yer scrawny butt and carries ya home ta feed her young."

Skeeter turned and gave one last look in our direction before he disappeared back into the cave. That left us nothing to do but wait. We figured an hour would be enough time to make sure Skeeter and the other Reb had fallen back asleep. The problem was neither one of us had a watch, not that we could see it at night anyhow.

Eli claimed he could tell what time it was by watching the moon arch across the night sky, but I kind of doubt that. We sat there listening to the sounds of the forest at night. It was an active place around midnight. Raccoons scurried passed us, bats swooped and sharp-eyed owls hooted.

I kept thinking I saw snakes crawling in the grass. Eli said I was spooked and told me to lie upon the log we were hiding behind so

I was off the ground. We were far enough from the outlaw cave that they could not see me even in the moonlight.

"You think we waited long enough?" I asked when the moon moved behind a tall tree.

"I reckon so."

With our makeshift rope halters in hand, we crept towards the horses. The corral was sturdy-built with tree saplings lashed together with leather straps. The fence sections were about twenty feet long and four feet high. Now Trooper could clear this fence without even taking a run up, but it was high enough to hold most stock.

"You get the pony," Eli whispered as we squeezed through the fence rails.

"Yeah, I know. You already told me."

I walked up slowly to Libby's pony and scratched her behind the ear as I had done many times before. Scarlett recognized me and I had no trouble putting the rope around her neck.

Eli was able to do the same with the sorrel mare. She was twenty years old and had been around us since we were kids. Eli handed me the rope on the sorrel mare and approached the dappled-gray filly. She had only been with us a few months and was not looking cooperative. As Eli walked toward her, she shied away, moving to the far end of the corral.

"Easy girl," Eli said softly. "It's gonna be okay."

Eli had always had a way with horses— "hosses", he called them. He moved towards her to place the loop over her head, and she dodged him and nickered softly. The sound made my stomach clinch; Skeeter had shown himself to be a light sleeper.

"Easy now, girl," he said soothingly. "You be ah good girl now."

He had about fifteen feet of rope and, when he got within eight feet of the filly, tossed it over her head. It settled around her neck, and I held my breath. *Please don't whinny*! She didn't. Eli reeled her in and she followed along behind him as he gently patted her neck.

When he got to the gate, he opened it with his left hand while softly saying calming things. I led the pony and the mare out of the corral, never taking my eyes off the outlaw cave. I pictured Skeeter charging out of the cave with his big pistol.

Eli took the lead and we headed into the little valley towards the water. Everything was going well until I let Libby's pony get too close to Mr. Tyler's filly. Shetlands have a reputation for having an ornery streak and the red pony was no exception. She nipped the filly on the rump, and it brought a quick reaction. The filly whinnied in protest and the sound traveled through the silence of the night.

"We gotta move," Eli rasped.

And move we did! We rushed down the narrow valley between the two sandhills and onto the beach. Without hesitation, with the horses in tow, we plunged into the dark water of Beaver Lake hoping we remembered where the narrow underwater ridge of sand was located. We didn't. By the time I was thirty feet from shore, I was up to my armpits in water and the red pony was starting to look frantic. I looked at Eli and the water was only up to his knees.

"Come towards me," said Eli. "The sand bar is this way."

I followed his lead and we were soon only ankle deep in water and moving towards the portion of the sand ridge that was above water; it was the small island with the wild cherry trees. We travelled quickly in the shallow water as we constantly glanced over our shoulders to see if Skeeter and his buddy Bill were following us. When we reached the shore, we collapsed on the beach and were barely able to hang on to the ropes that were around the necks of the horses.

"You suppose they are out there looking for us?"

Eli looked up at the moon before answering. "Must be 'bout one in the mornin'. Those varmits probably never even woke up."

"Do you really think so?"

"Naw, not really."

There was a moment of silence as what we had just done sank in.

"You think they can follow our tracks in the moonlight?"

"Maybe," he conceded, scratching his chin nervously. "That bein' the case, we gotta move ta the other end ah this island fer we tucker out and fall asleep."

Sleep. Did that ever sound good. I was so excited a few minutes ago and now it was all draining away, and I felt very sleepy. I fought off the feeling and grabbed the rope on the pony.

"I'll take the other two," said Eli. "You keep that ornery pony away from them. Don't need her biting them on the ass."

~

CHAPTER 15
The Getaway

I was awakened by a nudge on my shoulder. When I opened my eyes, the face of the red pony was less than a foot from mine. "Whoa!" It was a rude way to wake up.

The smaller island was covered with wild cherries and Scarlett had cleaned the ground around me and was now after what was under my shoulder. I sat up and stretched my arms skyward. The hardened sand was no match for my cozy featherbed at home. As thoughts of our escape from Bogus Island last night seeped into my sleepy brain, my pulse quickened, and I was on my feet.

The sun had barely risen above the horizon, but Bill and Skeeter had probably figured out the horses they had stolen were gone. I hoped they would search Bogus Island first, but criminals probably have their own way of doing things.

"Eli, come on. We gotta get moving."

He sat up immediately and was instantly awake.

"Yeah, we gotta get goin'," said Eli. "They'll foller the tracks down ta the water and be on us like buzzards on ah kilt rabbit."

The tracks. I had forgotten about all those tracks we left as we scurried down to the water. Skeeter and Bill might have seen them in the moonlight. Maybe they lit up a lantern and followed the tracks. They might be standing behind those cherry trees getting ready to pounce on us. I took several deep breaths trying to get my imagination under control.

"Ben, don't just stand there. Let's go."

I grabbed the lead rope on the red pony and followed Eli, who was already at the water's edge. He hesitated for a moment as he determined where the underwater pathway was.

"It'll be easier in the daylight," he said, pointing at the water to our left. "It's sand so ya can see where it's shallow. Over there is the underwater road."

He guided the sorrel mare and the gray filly to the spot some twenty feet away and, sure enough, the water was only up passed his ankles. I pulled the lead rope on the red pony and followed at a safe distance. I thought of putting on my wet shoes, but gave up that idea. I tied them together with the laces and hung them around my neck. I needed to let them dry out a little more before I put them back on. Wet leather shoes were bound to be uncomfortable and give you blisters. Eli had never taken off his deerskin moccasins and seemed alright with sloshing through the water with them on.

A morning fog was hanging on the water and we could hear flocks of birds flying overhead but we did not see them. I could not see the shore, but I remember that it was more than a mile away. We walked the narrow path back on the underwater sand bar until the morning sun burnt off the fog. When that happened, we were a few hundred yards from shore and the water was up past our knees.

"Sand bars disappearin'," said Eli. "We gotta find that underwater bridge them outlaws built."

The sand ridge had been light and visible, but the sunken logs were as dark as the water, so we had to feel our way along. At least we could see the shore now. My father always said that men became criminals because they were too lazy to work, but even he would have had to admit the underwater log bridge required a lot of effort and determination.

"You think all the hard work it took to build this," I said. "If these varmints would have put that towards honest employment, they'd been better off."

"My Grandpappy said some men would rather make uh dollar dishonestly than two dollars honestly. There just ain't no explainin' some folks."

As I thought about the strange nature of mankind, I strayed too close to the edge and slipped off the bridge and into the deeper water. I went in up to my eyeballs and began treading water.

"Ben, you alright?" Eli was there quickly extending a helping hand.

"Damn, I got my shoes wet again."

"Heck, you got everything wet. Better watch where you're steppin', tenderfoot."

I removed the shoes from around my neck and flung them to Eli. He caught them at the knot in the laces that joined them together. I was embarrassed and ignored his helping hand. I swam back and climbed onto the bridge myself. I don't know why I thought that would help me save face. When I stood up angry and dripping wet, Eli began to laugh.

"It's okay, Ben. These logs are slippery as goose grease. Coulda happened ta anybody."

But it didn't happen to anyone, it happened to me. Soaked, I trudged the last hundred feet to the shore and sat down in the sand.

Eli disappeared into the bushes that lined the broad, sandy beach and emerged a few minutes later with two large branches.

"What are those for?"

"We gotta wipe out our tracks this time."

He dropped one by me as he headed for the water. It hit me in the head on the way down. That was the way my day was going so far. Eli started at the water and began sweeping the leafy branch back and forth making the hoof marks disappear in the loose sand.

"Take the horses and get'em off the beach and into the bushes," Eli instructed. He threw my wet shoes at me. I was tempted to try and put them back on as I pulled the horses into the bulrushes by the shore. I thought about the rattlesnake I had encountered the night before and didn't relish the idea of walking into the brush barefooted. My high-top shoes at least came up above my ankles and would provide me with a little protection.

"How's that look?" asked Eli after he completed his task and joined me in the bushes.

"It's like we were never here."

I started to pull the horses back on the beach and Eli grabbed the reins.

"We can't go back on the beach yet. We gotta go north ah ways through these cattails and scrub fer it's safe ta go back on the beach. They could be up on that sand hill with a spyglass lookin' fer us on that nice white beach. We'd stick out like colored folks at a Klan meetin'."

Now that was an interesting way to put it. There was an organization called the Ku Klux Klan making a name for itself around Tennessee. It seems a lot of southern soldiers weren't happy about how the war turned out and General Nathan Bedford Forrest was assembling them into a secret army. This would not be good news for Hopkins Park. The folks there were mainly ex-slaves that were allowed to purchase land there because it was so sandy no one else wanted it. The small community had been a regular stop of the Underground Railroad.

Eli sat on a clump of dry grass and rested a moment. I sat next to him and attempted to put my shoes on. I turned each upside down and water ran out of them.

"I can't get my shoes back on. They're wet. I don't want to be tracking through the swamp grass back here barefooted. I already met a rattlesnake. Don't want to run into a water moccasin without my high tops on."

"Well, ride the pony. She's use ta you, ain't she?"

It was true that Libby and I had taken turns riding Scarlett, but that did not mean that the cantankerous little pony had taken a shine to me. Nevertheless, I threw my leg over the ill-tempered Shetland and hopped aboard. Her only reaction was a snort of disapproval.

Eli chose to remain on foot, leading the mare and the dappled-gray filly, picking his way through the reeds and scrub grass. He avoided bare patches of sand that would leave tracks that could easily be followed. I rode behind, keeping Scarlett a safe distance away from the other horses so she wouldn't cause any mischief. The sun was up now and the marsh was alive with activity; birds were chirping and insects were buzzing. When we had gone about half a mile, Eli pulled the horses towards the beach.

"Guess we dun picked our way through the swamp long enough," he said. "Let's go back to the beach and we'll make better time."

I could tell he was getting tired of picking his way through the underbrush. From my vantage point on the pony, I could better see through the swaying bulrush growing in the watery backwaters of the lake. I had a view down the sandy beach before we ventured upon it.

"Eli, stop."

"What?" He sounded irritated with my blunt command.

"There are riders coming up the beach."

He rushed forward and pushed the cattails apart for a better view. There were two men coming from the south. When they came to the underwater bridge, they turned right and entered the water.

"They didn't even dismount," I said. "They knew exactly where the underwater bridge was."

"Not their first time through, I'd guess."

"Who do you suppose they are?"

Eli scratched his chin and pondered this for a moment as he watched the riders progress towards the first island.

"Didn't those two varmits on the island say somethin' bout ah feller they called the Major. He was the one that'd come ta get the hosses."

"Yeah. He was the one supposed to pick up the horses and take them away to sell them."

"I'd guess one ah those fellers ta be him."

~

CHAPTER 16
Back at Camp

Gray Wolf seemed to be twenty years younger as he described his actions on the night before. He was excited as he told us about the bullet whizzing by his head and he showed us where one had hit the prowl of his canoe. The night of danger had reawakened the warrior in him, and he was moving with a spring in his step.

"Your flaming arrows did the trick," I told him. "Those two rascals didn't see us slip onto the island. We just waited until after midnight and took off with the horses." I didn't bother telling him about the rattlesnake or the red pony causing problems.

No use bringing up what went wrong. He was an adult that thinks we know what we're doing. I didn't want him to start worrying about us and think about turning us in before the job is done. We still had to figure out how to get Trooper back and we might need his help again.

Gray Wolf joined us around the morning fire, sitting on a stump and looking very satisfied. He had killed a rabbit and cooked it on a spit over the open flames. Eli and I picked at the hot, juicy meat. I never cared for rabbit. I thought it had a gamey taste, but this small feast was delicious.

Gray Wolf's camp resembled a walled fortress in a way. He had cleared the high ground in the middle of an acre or two of tall reeds. The entrance was a curved path that made a partial loop and did not give away the location of his secret camp. The cleared area at the center was a circle about fifty feet in diameter. In the middle of the clearing was his lean-to dwelling and a firepit with a spit over it. I noticed that he used dried oak logs because hardwood gave off very little smoke that would give away the location of his hidden camp.

Besides coveting my father's binoculars, Gray Wolf also took a shine to Maggie, the sorrel mare. She had always been a friendly horse that was eager to please. Eli and I had both learned to ride on her. She was a little spavin in the hocks now that she was twenty years old. I guess Gray Wolf and Maggie were about the same age in horse years. Maybe that was part of the old mare's appeal to him.

Eli was kneeling by the fire. He got up and walked over to where Gray Wolf was scratching the mare behind her ear.

"Ya want ta take her fer ah ride?"

I was surprised at this proposal and wished Eli would have run it by me first. If the old fellow falls off the horse and is injured, what are we going to do with him out in the middle of the marsh? We would have to get Dr. Shronts and then he would turn us over to the sheriff for a return to Momence.

The suggestion of a ride did bring a twinkle to the old warrior's eyes. He removed the rope from around Maggie's neck and fashioned an Indian-style halter which he slipped over her head.

"Once I had a fine horse many years ago. I would race her down the beach."

It was my understanding that there was no beach around Beaver Lake until Puett attempted to drain the lake in 1852. That would mean that Gray Wolf was galloping around the lake ten, maybe fifteen years ago, so it hadn't been that long. Maybe I was underestimating his horsemanship. If Eli was willing to give the old warrior a chance, so was I.

Gray Wolf crossed over to the left side of the horse and contemplated how he was going to mount the mare. Indians did not use saddles but sprang onto the backs of their ponies like agile cats. We knew Gray Wolf was not up for that, so Eli bent over slightly and clasped his hands together to form a stirrup for the old warrior to step into and mount. Gray Wolf looked insulted by this and led Maggie over to the stump I had been sitting on. He stepped up and threw his leg over the mare. Problem solved. He looked pleased with himself.

Gray Wolf nudged his heels into Maggie's side and guided her to the entrance. He coaxed her into a trot and disappeared around the curve.

"Do you think he's going to be alright?"

"Sure," was Eli's confident reply. He walked over to Gray Wolf's canoe and examined the bullet hole in the prowl. "If he got this war canoe in here by himself, he must still be pretty strong."

I got up and walked over to the Indian canoe. We found some little round logs around the canoe and figured he used them as rollers to move it around. It must have taken considerable time for Gray Wolf to pull the heavy canoe from the ditch to his camp. Eli was right. The old man still had a lot of grit and determination.

Libby's canoe was turned upside down next to the birch bark canoe and the gash had been expertly repaired. I had to admit it looked on the light side next to Gray Wolf's canoe.

"I guess he's sprier than we think," said Eli.

We went back and sat by the fire and pulled off chunks of the rabbit. We savored each bite and relaxed after our previous night that was full of excitement, but little sleep.

"You think the folks in town are out lookin' fer ya?" asked Eli. "We been out here three days now."

"Looking for us, you mean."

"Ain't no search party out lookin' fer me."

"I think Libby will keep her mouth shut like she promised," I said, "but that guy talking to Doctor Shronts said he was going to send a telegram to Momence asking about us."

"Those two Rebs are the search party we gotta be worried 'bout."

Eli had no sooner got those words out of his mouth than Gray Wolf came galloping into camp. The look on his weathered face told us something was wrong.

"Riders," he announced, "coming up beach."

"How many?" I asked.

"Four," he said, holding up four fingers to make sure we understood.

Eli jumped up and kicked sand on the fire. He started to go out the pathway Gray Wolf had provided but changed his mind and headed directly south into the dense wall of reeds. As he pushed his way through them, I grabbed the binoculars and followed in his path.

When we got near the beach, we parted the reeds carefully and peeked out. There were four riders, all right. They were about a half a mile away and not moving in any hurry. Gray Wolf must have amazing eyesight for his age.

We each took a turn looking through the glasses and concluded that two were Skeeter and his buddy Bill from the island. There was another guy wearing a coonskin hat that was out front, looking down as he rode. He got off for a closer look at the hoofprints our horses had made in the sand. He turned towards another man sitting rail-straight in the saddle and told him something. The man was wearing what looked like a campaign hat that a cavalry officer might wear.

"You suppose those are the two fellows we saw heading for the island this morning?" I asked.

"I reckon."

"That must be the Major they were talking about last night."

"The guy in the coonskin hat picked up our trail, that's fer sure. He must be ah tracker. Let's get outah here."

We picked our way through the path in the reeds we had created to get back to the camp. I was glad to see Gray Wolf had not dismounted so we didn't have to put him back on Maggie. We could not leave him here because the guy in the coonskin hat would soon lead them to this camp. Me and Eli mounted up and we all rode north out of the trail through the reeds. Eli dismounted and found a branch to try covering our tracks.

"Eli, I don't think that is going to throw them off."

"Yeah, you're probably right," he conceded, tossing the branch aside. "Let's go find Trooper."

"What! We need to just run for home."

"You got me into this. Now ya wanna quit?"

"Well, that was before we had four guys with guns following us."

I could not believe five days ago I was trying to talk him into this crazy idea. I had forgotten what it was like when Eli got a notion to do something in his head. He had no quit in him. There was nothing for me to do except get ready for action and hope everything turned out okay.

"Gray Wolf, do you know where we can find Mike Shafer?" I asked.

The old man looked at me and then Eli. His furrowed brow showed his concern.

"Mike Shafer is very bad man. No horse worth going against him."

"Well, Trooper ain't no ordinary hoss," said Eli, "and he's gonna win us a lot of money. Fer half of ah thousand dollars, I'll go up against the devil himself."

I had dangled the thousand-dollar purse in front of Eli to get him to come on this mission. I felt some misgivings now that he had fixed his mind upon it. We were kids. What if they said we couldn't enter the race? Eli wasn't a white kid either. Him riding in the race was going to rub some fellers wrong.

Gray Wolf thought about this for a moment then nodded his agreement. Considering he was fighting at the Battle of

Tippecanoe when he was our age, it probably wasn't that crazy to him. He nudged the sorrel mare in the ribs and we were off. The red pony had to take a lot of extra steps to keep up with the bigger horses, but she was determined. Scarlett didn't like to see another horse out in front of her.

~

CHAPTER 17
Poor Sam Patch

When we got to the ditch, we heard a horse coming fast and we reined in our mounts. Then there was a commotion and a horse whinnying in distress. Me and Eli dismounted and approached the ditch stealthily to see what was going on. *Could it be the four men from the island?* How could they have come so far so fast?

We peeked out through the reeds on the bank and saw a young man lying in the ditch just the other side of Gray Wolf's dam. He was holding his left leg and a large horse covered with muddy water was trotting away from him. He tried to get up and the leg would not hold him. He fell back into the slime-covered water.

"Damn it all! I'm a dead man now!"

He was young, maybe a couple years older than Eli, and was not one of the riders we had watched coming up the beach. Me and Eli slid down the side of the earthen dam and approached him cautiously. He was wearing a long coat and we could not tell if he was armed. He looked up at us, startled.

"Where'd you fellas come from?"

"You all right?" I asked, ignoring his question about our sudden appearance.

"Hell, no! Believe I done busted my leg."

His accent was southern like the men on the island. When he tried to sit up, his coat flopped open and I saw the gun strapped to his waist. I glanced up at Eli and he saw it too. *Had we missed him on the island?*

"Let's get ya outah this water," said Eli, grabbing him by the shoulders. As he did, he motioned with his head for me to pull the gun. I just froze and the moment passed. Eli gave me an exasperated look and stood behind the mystery man, ready to pounce on him if he made a wrong move.

"Thank ya, boys," he said as he laid back on the bank of the ditch, grimacing in pain. His words of appreciation took the edge off the situation and Eli moved out from behind him, his eyes still on the gun.

"I got in too big ah hurry and my horse slid coming down that bank and fell on me." He finally sat up with great effort and looked down at his bent left leg. "Pretty sure it's broke. It's the end ah the line fer poor Sam Patch. If'n I didn't have bad luck, I wouldn't have no luck at all."

"You're going to be all right," I assured him. "There's a doctor that lives a few miles from here on the river. We can take you to him."

Eli looked at me and shook his head to nix that idea. I had spoken too soon. We were on the run and had to take care of ourselves first.

"We gotta get moving, buddy," said Eli. "We'll send the doctor back fer ya."

"Yeah, you'd best get outah here. There be some bad men comin' after me and ya don't be needin' ta get caught up in my mess."

Eli looked at me curiously. I asked the question that was on both our minds.

"Are these men from Bogus Island?"

Now Sam Patch looked at us curiously.

"That they be. I was one of their ranks ah few months ago, but got tired ah their thievin' ways. I took that there horse over yonder and lit out. Now the Major and his boys are comin' down the beach this way ta get me and get that horse. I'll have hell ta pay. I just hope he kills me quick and don't throw my body in one ah those black bogs."

The horse he was referring to was standing in the middle of the ditch fifty yards away. His head was hanging down and the

125

reins from his bridle were dragging in the stagnant water. The big horse glanced at us, and then quickly looked away as though he knew he had done something wrong.

"I don't think they're after you," I said, hoping to take him out of his dark mood. "Me and Eli here relieved them of all the horses we're now riding. I believe this mysterious major is after us."

"Damn. Don't that beat all," he said with a laugh. "Sounds like we're all in the same pot ah stew."

"Well, I don't think stealing your own horses back from thieves is a crime, but I don't know how they will look at it."

"The way the Major looks at it, it is. He has commandeered those horses for the Confederacy, and they are no longer yer property."

"That's crazy," said Eli.

"With that line of thinking," I said, "we are all in the same pot of stew. We're Horse thieves."

"Yep, the Major's likely hang us all."

We had given Gray Wolf the binoculars and he was our lookout. He had remained on the mare at our insistence. We did not want to help the old warrior to remount. Eli had convinced him that he would be of more value staying on top of his dam and reporting on whether the Major and his party were coming our way.

"Ya see anybody comin'?" Eli shouted up to him. Gray Wolf shook his head side-to-side to indicate there was not. We were safe for the moment.

"I figure them rascals would be headin' down the ditch after us already," said Eli. "We sure left enough tracks leadin' them this way."

"Yeah," I said. "That guy in the coonskin hat sure appeared to be a tracker."

"That man be called Gib and he's one hell of a tracker," Sam assured us.

We spent a few precious moments trying to figure out their lack of interest in us.

Eli asked me, "Didn't the lame one say the Major was gonna be fumin' mad cause they took Trooper to Mike Shafer ta give'im ah new look?"

"Who's Trooper?" asked Sam Patch.

"He's my family's stallion," I said. "Fastest horse in the county."

"Maybe the whole damn state. I'm gonna ride him in a race next month and win us a thousand bucks."

"Maybe that's why they ain't comin' this way," said Sam. "The Major most likely already got ah buyer fer ah horse like thet. He's got rich gentlemen in St. Louie give a lot of dough fer a horse thet fast. Shippin' him out thet far away, ain't no need ah changin' his markings."

"Well, if they are not coming for us, that's a blessing." I thought saying that might boost morale.

"Not much ah one," countered Eli. "We was on the way ourselves ta get Trooper back from Old Shaf."

"Yes, now we have competition," I said. Our competition has guns and we do not, however.

"Well, they're gonna get thar first," Sam assured us. "They won't come down this ditch. Comes to close to Lake Village. The Major will stay clear of ah town full ah Yankees. They'll go as far east as they can on the beach and then go up ah secret trail up ta Shafer's ridge. I went with'em there once a'fore. The trail's on high ground. No black bogs or quicksand ta worry 'bout."

"Yeah, they won't have to fight the marsh every step of the way." I was about to ask him if he could lead us to this secret trail, but I caught myself. *He's got a broken leg.*

"Well, I hate ta be ah bother," said Sam Patch, grimacing. "But could you fellas get thet doctor ya'll was tellin' me about?"

Eli thought a moment before coming up with an idea. "Gray Wolf fixed up Libby's canoe. We can put Sam here in it and pull him down ta the river and over ta Doc Shronts."

Now I thought that was a particularly good idea and wish it had occurred to me.

"We would be killing two birds with one stone," I said. "We'd get Sam to the doctor without going out of our way and we could just pick up the canoe on our way back to Momence." *That is, if we make it back*. I pushed that depressing thought out of my mind.

"Ben, if ya can go fetch his hoss," said Eli. "I'll go back ta Gray Wolf's camp and get the canoe."

That seemed reasonable since Eli was stronger than me and could portage that canoe much faster than I could. The trouble was, he would be the better one to go fetch the horse too. Eli had a special way with horses.

Sam Patch's horse was a reddish-brown fella, called a roan in horse lingo. He was a large gelding, maybe sixteen hands or better. Sam had assured me that, being a gelding, he was pretty calm and easy to manage. There was talk of having Trooper gelded before he reached his first birthday, but he was turning out to be such a fine specimen of horse flesh that my father knew we would be approached to rent him out for stud. Then the war came and those plans, like so many other things, were lost in the chaos.

Sam's assurances were correct. I walked right up to the big horse and took the reins that were hanging in the nasty ditch water. By the time I led the gelding back to where Sam was lying in pain, Eli appeared at the top of the dam with the canoe.

"Here it comes," he announced as he slipped it down the bank towards us. I caught the bow and pulled it next to Sam. When Eli made it down the bank, we bent down and each grabbed a shoulder.

"This is gonna hurt, ain't it?" I think Sam already knew the answer to that.

"Not as much as if we tried to put you on a horse," I said.

We yanked him up and he let out a howl as the injured leg pressed against the ground. We switched things around and Eli held him up by himself while I gently lifted his leg. Sam wasn't that big, maybe five foot-eight and a hundred and twenty pounds. I would guess living off the land in the marsh would tend to keep a fella on the scrawny side.

Once we had him in the canoe, Sam's breathing slowed down a bit and he tried to smile at us through the pain. It was weird holding his leg because it was at such a strange angle. I didn't see any blood seeping out of his pant leg, so I guess it wasn't shattered and poking through the skin. I wasn't about to peel back his Levi's and find out. I would let Doc Shronts handle that chore.

Sam's horse was the only one with a saddle on it, so Eli fastened the rope attached to the canoe to the gelding's saddle horn and led it down the ditch. Before we left, Eli talked Gray Wolf into digging a little notch in his dam and letting some more water into the ditch.

The water was only an inch deep in places and we didn't want to chance ripping the new patch off the bottom. Just a little water went a long way in letting the canoe glide to reach the Kankakee River. Gray Wolf's dam was somewhere around the half-way point of the five-mile ditch, so it would be about two and a half miles to the river.

~

CHAPTER 18
Up the River

The long haul to the river was not easy on poor Sam Patch. Even with the extra water that flowed from slightly opening the dam, the canoe still hit bottom occasionally in the shallow ditch, and Sam made sure to tell us it was causing him pain. When we reached the river, he looked up at us and smiled weakly.

"I rode mules over the mountains, and it were ah smoother ride than this."

"Well, the tough parts over," Eli assured him. "Yer gonna be floatin' down the river now. Smooth as glass, I'd say."

We waited for Gray Wolf to catch up and he and Eli swam the horses across the river. Eli rode into the water on the dappled gray filly trailing Sam's horse behind. He tied the stirrups to the saddle horn so the fenders would not get wet. Gray Wolf trailed Scarlett behind Maggie.

The old mare had dealt with the ornery pony on many occasions. Scarlett knew if she nipped Maggie on the rump, retribution would be quick and severe. I was given the task of paddling the canoe up the river to Doctor Shronts. With Sam sprawled out in the bottom of the canoe, there wasn't much room for anyone else. I was the smallest, so I got the job.

Sam was lying towards the back of the canoe, so I was allowed three feet in the bow. Paddling from the front in such a confined space did not make it easy to steer, but we did not want to move Sam again. He had been through a lot of pain and gliding on the smooth water of the river was a relief.

His head started rolling from side-to-side and his eyes fluttered and closed. Somewhere I had heard it was best to keep an injured person awake, so I was determined to do so until we got to the doctor's place. Coming up with small talk when you absolutely had to was more difficult than I thought.

"So, how did you fall in with that gang of horse thieves?" *A little awkward, but definitely a conversation starter.*

Sam pulled his head off the bottom of the canoe and looked at me through pain filled eyes. "I had ta get outah Tennessee and headin' up north with these fellas seemed like ah good idear at the time." He sucked in a deep breath as though saying this had been a tremendous effort.

"Why did you have to leave Tennessee?"

"I didn't want ta join the Klan. I already been forced into the Confederate Army ta fight fer somethin' I didn't believe in. None ah my kin had any slaves. We was poor dirt farmers."

"The war is over, Sam. Nobody could force you to join the Klan."

Sam looked at me like I was some babe in the woods. "You Yankees up here think the war is over. It ain't. General Nate's puttin' together his army. Three fellers from my old company caught me and put ah gun ta my head. Told me I was joining or else. Thet's when I lit out north."

Well, as you can imagine, this came as quite a shock to me. I was surprised to find ex-rebs hanging out in the swamp and stealing from near-by towns in the name of the Confederacy. Now Sam tells me the Klan is forming up a secret army in Tennessee. I know some folks don't take kindly to losing, but this war has taken too much from so many folks. It took my father. This war that sometime pitted brother against brother needed to end.

Sam laid his head back down in the bottom of the canoe. All the talking had sapped what energy he had left. We had spent the morning dragging him in the canoe the two miles or more to the river. The sun was now high in the sky, and it was turning out to be a very warm day at the end of May. Sam's eyes rolled back, and he went into a delirious half sleep. He began talking out of his head.

"No, Captain. We ain't ah gonna charge thet fence. Them Yanks got cannons and are shootin' grapeshot. Ya see what happened ta the first wave ya sent out there. Ever one ah them boys is ah layin' out thar dead."

From his deliriums, I got the idea that Sam had been part of some mutiny. That might be another explanation of why such a seemingly nice fella had thrown in with horse thieves and ended up in the outlaw country of Indiana.

"He all right?" Eli wanted to know. "What's he yellin' 'bout?"

Eli was on the north bank of the river riding about thirty feet from me. We were at a bend in the river with a flat, sandy shore that allowed him to ride close to the water.

"He's been in pain for quite some time," I said. "Starting to talk out of his head about the war."

135

Sam Patch was carrying around a lot of pain from the war between the states. A doctor could set a broken leg and it would mend, but there wasn't any doctor to deal with horrible memories that wouldn't let him be. Maybe someday there would be doctors that could help men like Sam Patch and Libby's dad, Major Carter. Maybe someday, but not right now.

"Try ta keep him awake," Eli shouted out to me. "Doc Shronts's cabin be just around this bend in the river."

Eli's memory served him well. As soon as the river straighten, I could see the doctor's cabin a little ways up on the left. There was smoke coming from the chimney and that was a welcome site. That meant he was home. My fear was that we would get here and he would be gone; maybe down to Lake Village or worst, all the way back to Momence.

Eli and Gray Wolf galloped ahead and by the time I had paddled to the cabin, they had Doctor Shronts out by the riverbank waiting. When I reached the water's edge, there were three pairs of eager hands ready to pull me onto the shore. Sam looked around wildly, confused by all this activity. He looked pale and clammy; sweat was running down his face and dripping off his chin. The doctor gave me a clean cloth and told me to dip it into the cool water of the river. When I brought it back, he put it on Sam's forehead while talking to him in soothing tones.

Doctor Shront's had us help pick up the canoe. Eli and I took the bow, and the doctor and Gray Wolf lifted the stern. When we put Sam down next to the cabin, the doctor whispered calming words in his ear as he loosened all of Sam's clothing. I continued to bring towels soaked in cool water to put on his head. When Sam's color improved and his rapid heart rate went down, Doctor Shronts had us lift him out of the canoe and bring him into the cabin.

The doctor gently cradled the injured leg, and we put Sam on the table in the middle of the main room. The doctor produced a large pair of scissors and urged us to keep talking to Sam. When the pants leg fell away, I saw the broken bone and caught myself before I threw up. It pushed against the skin at a sharp angle, but luckily did not break through. An open wound being in slimy ditch water would probably invite an infection.

Doctor Shronts took a bottle of whiskey down from a shelf and poured drinks for he and Sam. They began talking about living in the marsh and all the challenges it presented. Sam knocked back a second shot of whiskey; the doctor had not touched his. He told Sam the old story of the hunter who shot one deer and a second deer passing behind the first was dropped with the same bullet.

Sam laughed at this tale and admitted game was so thick he had brought down two birds with one shot last month. The doctor motioned with his head for me and Eli to get closer and I figured out where all the good-natured comradery was going.

"Sam, it's time to get down to business," he announced, still smiling. "Here, clamp your teeth down on this piece of wood. This is going to hurt a might."

The doctor motioned for us to hold him down and he quickly grabbed the leg and pulled it straight. I was amazed at how fast he set the bone back in place. Sam bellowed like a stuck hog.

He was gripping my arm so tight he was cutting off the circulation. He gave the doctor a look of betrayal, but I'm sure that feeling would pass when the pain eased up. Doctor Shronts gave him another shot of whiskey and he downed it eagerly. When the doctor was sure the pain had eased, he wrapped the injured leg with a piece of blanket.

"I need two of those flat, wood slats by the fireplace."

Eli was the closest and quickly began looking for two pieces of wood suitable for making a splint.

"Ben, go out to your canoe. I noticed you had a rope on the bow. Cut me three pieces about two foot long."

I was gone in a flash. I took out my trusty pocketknife and cut the pieces of rope to the required length. The task took longer than I thought it would because my knife had not been sharpened in a while.

When I got back inside, Eli had already supplied the slats for the splint, and they were waiting on me. While Eli held the slats in place, the doctor took the rope and tied a tightly drawn overhand knot followed by a square knot. With the splint solidly in place, Eli motioned with his head towards the door.

~

CHAPTER 19
Time to Ride

I walked out on the porch and saw Eli tying the red pony to an oak tree, giving it enough rope that it could graze. Gray Wolf was standing on a stump trying to maneuver Maggie into a position where he could mount her. The old mare obliged him, and he was able to swing his leg over and get on board. He pulled her rein to the left and rode over to where I was standing on the porch.

"We go now," he announced, pointing up at the sun. It was well passed mid-day and I understood his concern. We needed to find Mike Shafer's "studio" before dark and see if we could manage to liberate Trooper before the outlaws from Bogus Island took him. Thinking of Mike Shafer's reputation, maybe it would be easier to take the black stallion from the Major and his band of thieves.

Eli was mounted on the dappled-gray filly and brought the horse Sam had been riding for me. "Let's vamoose before the doctor comes out here."

"Shouldn't we at least say good-bye. We're sorta sticking him with Sam."

"He comes out here, he's gonna try ta stop us. He'll keep us here fer the sheriff just like he tried to do the last time. The sheriff will take us back ta Momence and we'll never see Trooper again."

He was right. That is probably how it would go. I wasted no time mounting Sam's big gelding. We broke into a gallop as we rode east along the river. Doctor Shronts most likely heard this and was standing on the porch waving for us to come back. For that reason, I didn't turn around and look.

It felt good to be sitting in a saddle again. Gray Wolf and Eli were accustomed to riding bareback, but I like the secure feeling of being in the cradle of a saddle. My feet were in the stirrups and one hand was on the saddle horn. With Eli's long legs, he clung to the sides of the filly like a spider. I would never be the rider that he was.

We rode east on a trail worn by travelers following the river. When we got north of Lake Village, we saw fishing shacks assembled by the water. Lake Village was situated between the Kankakee River and Beaver Lake. According to our town postmaster, Lake Village wasn't a real town, just a bunch of people living close together. He said to be a real town, it had to have a post office. He's an employee of the government of the United States, so I guess he should know what he's talking about. He said that Morocco, south of the lake, was the only real town in the marsh country of Indiana. Mr. Trowbridge said that it was not named for the place in Africa, but for boots made of Moroccan leather. Towns seem to come by their names in peculiar ways in the Midwest.

"Hey," said Eli, "someone's comin'." He was riding ahead of me. Gray Wolf was in the lead since he knew where Mike Shafer's "studio" was located.

Yes, there was someone coming down the river in a rowboat, a fishing pole draped over the side. The man was middle-aged and wearing a coat though it was a warm afternoon in May. I doubt if he was cold so maybe it was to keep the mosquitoes off. I had swatted maybe a dozen already today.

"Hello, the shore," he shouted when he was about fifty feet away.

"Good afternoon, sir." I finally answered even though I was riding drag. Gray Wolf and Eli just eyed him suspiciously.

"Yes, a wonderful afternoon. Summer's finally here." I noticed a slight hint of the South in his voice. He seemed a decent sort by first impression, but he could be a flimflam man and part of the gang of ex-rebs that now occupied Bogus Island.

"Yes, it's a nice day," I said, returning the pleasantries. Eli looked back at me, his eyes telling me to be careful what I say.

"Are you travelling far, lad?" the man asked me directly. Now he was eyeballing Gray Wolf and Eli suspiciously. Turning the situation around, he might just be a concerned citizen wondering why a young boy like myself was riding through the marsh with an old Indian and an older boy, who by his appearance, might well be a half-breed.

"So where are you headed, son?" This question was more pointed. I saw Eli was ready to tell him to move on.

"Roselawn," is what popped out of my mouth. Somewhere I had heard of another settlement further east that was centered around a general store run by a Mr. Rose. "We have business there," I added for good measure.

I saw Eli smile at my quick lie and the tension seemed to ease.

"Yes, this is my Indian guide and his grandson," I continued. "My father hired them to take me there safely." Eli looked at me with raised eyebrows now. Don't overdo it was the message.

"Ah, Roselawn. I heard they are thinking of incorporating just like we intend to do here in Lake Village. This savage swamp is going to be civilized soon. We need to drain that damn lake though so we can turn it into farmland. Henry Rainford is our best ditcher. He will make short work of Beaver Lake."

Both Eli and I looked at Gray Wolf. The old warrior took the news stoically and his face revealed nothing. Only his eyes showed defiance as he looked upon the man in the boat.

"Why do ya wanna drain the lake fer farmland?" asked Eli. "That lake bottom's sand. Can't grow much in sand. I know. I'm from Hopkins Park. It's sandy there."

The man in the boat gave Eli a long appraising look.

"My name is John Bunch," the man said, after a moment of silence. He apparently felt it proper to introduce himself. "I came here from the South before the war. I didn't agree with the Confederate cause, and I heard they were about to lynch me."

"Why'd ya come here?" asked Eli. I guess he was now convinced John Bunch was not one of the island outlaws.

"Well, being a Southerner, I had to worry about my safety in the North too. I heard of the swamp country in Indiana where there were few people and the law seldom visited."

"That's true," said Eli. "Nobody asks too many questions of ah man out here."

"Yes, that is what originally brought me here. I used to stay in that fish shack over there." He turned in his boat to point to a sad looking structure about a hundred yards away in a bayou just off the river. "Now that the war is over, I moved right into the village. My neighbor was a Yankee soldier. We get along just fine."

Eli nodded towards the east and jiggled the reins of the filly. I got the message. Time to go. "Well, it was real nice talking with you, Mr. Bunch, but we got to go now, or we will never make Roselawn by sunset."

"You boys be careful now. You're gonna pass real close to the residence of the outlaw Mike Shafer. He's a bad one. You don't want to cross paths with him."

"Thank you for the advice, sir." Eli and Gray Wolf were already about fifty feet up the trail. I clucked at the gelding and nudged him in the ribs to catch up.

We rode for about a mile before Gray Wolf turned Maggie into the river at a ford that was evident only to him. The river bottom was firm there, but the water came up to touch the stirrups of the big gelding. Gray Wolf picked up a trail on the other side of the river that was not well travelled. We had to frequently duck under overhanging branches and vines, and in some spots, we could barely tell where the path was because of weeds growing over it.

After a ways, we rode up a ridge that ran east to west in the marsh. This must be "Shafer's Ridge", named for the famous bad-man himself. We came to another pathway and Gray Wolf turned left on it. It was well used, and I began to feel very nervous when I realized this was the trail that Mike Shafer used for his coming and going. Then I saw it. In the middle of the trail was a pile of fresh "horse apples." Someone had just passed this way.

~

CHAPTER 20
On Shafer's Ridge

Eli dismounted and examined the green pile of horse manure. Then he inspected the many hoof prints that scarred up the trail. "Looks like two, maybe three riders came up that rise over there." He pointed to an overgrown, but still visible trail, that was to our right and intersected the well-used pathway that we were now on.

Gray Wolf examined the tracks as he looked down from the back of the mare and raised three fingers. That made it more definite. So, was this the secret passage that Sam Patch told us about? The trail that Mike Shafer and the Bogus Island outlaws used to bring horses back and forth. It would make sense that the Major and his band of ex-rebs arrived here on Shafer Ridge before us. We had to take Sam Patch to Doctor Shronts. But we had seen four coming down the beach. *Where was the fourth rider?*

We rode cautiously on towards a bend in the trail not knowing what was around it. Then we heard a woman yelling at the top of her lungs. Eli was quickly off his horse and hurrying ahead on foot. He stopped behind an oak tree and peeked around the corner.

"They're here," was his only message when he returned. Eli grabbed the reins of the filly and led it into a gulley. He motioned for us to follow. I fell in behind Gray Wolf and Maggie. I was confused at first, but then realized he was cutting the corner of the bend in the trail. When we were close enough to see the peak of a barn roof, he handed the filly's reins to Gray Wolf and told me to do the same. Eli motioned for Gray Wolf to take the horses to the rear. I could see the sense in that because if we had to flee quickly, we did not have time to help Gray Wolf back on Maggie. The hope was, of course, that he would remain mounted. The old warrior could ride like the wind, but that was after you boosted him aboard.

Eli and I crept forward through the pucker bush and scrub grass until we were at the edge of a barnyard. There was a sturdy-built log cabin with store-bought glass windows. Out of one of the windows a teenage girl was watching her mother who was standing on the makeshift porch; the woman was holding a shotgun. In the middle of the barnyard was the Major, still mounted and holding the reins of two other horses.

"Madam, the black stallion is mine and I intend to take him."

"You ain't taking nothin' til my man gets back," she said resolutely. "Now tell them two galoots ya brung with ya ta get out of our barn."

The barn she spoke of was more of a lean-to with a corral on the open end. The two "galoots" she was referring to were probably our friends from Bogus Island— Skeeter and his buddy Bill.

"Ain't nobody taken the horse 'til the work is paid for," the woman continued. "Mike spent considerable time on that stallion."

"The stallion does not require any altering of his appearance. I am taking it to St. Louis to sell to a gentleman willing to pay five hundred dollars for him. There is a time limit. I must have him there in three days."

The Major sounded very educated and had no accent that I could detect. He was probably from a wealthy Southern family and attended a university in the North. My father had told me the top Confederate officers were from money families because they had to supply their own uniforms and horses. They were appointed by each state's governor, so they had to be well-connected.

"I don't care nothin' about yer time limit," the woman said with a sneer. "Ya ain't takin' that big horse 'til my man gets back. He'll skin me alive if'un he comes home and that horse is gone."

And then he was there! It was as though I blinked, and Mike Shafer appeared in the middle of the barnyard. He was of above average height and powerfully built. Graying black hair made me think he was in his fifties, but he moved so smoothly it was hard to tell. He was not old, but I had heard his nickname, Old Shaf, was a tribute to his cunning.

"Mike, this here fancy gentleman says he wants that big stallion and he wants it now. He needs to get him to St. Louie in three days. Says a man gonna give'm five hundred dollars. Never heard of one horse worth that much."

Old Shaf waved his hand to signal silence. "Yeah. I heard all that."

"Shall I assume you are Mr. Shafer?" asked the Major.

"Yer talkin' to him."

"My boys didn't get their orders straight. They were not supposed to bring him over here to your famous 'studio' for work. I'm taking him all the way to St. Louis so no disguising markings will be necessary.

I will pay you for whatever work you have done."

At this moment Bill emerged from the barn with Skeeter close behind him. The gimpy little reb was leading Trooper. It had taken both of them to put a bridle on the big stallion. One of the horses the Major was holding had moved in the way and they did not see Mike Shafer.

"Major, he put ah boiled tater on his forehead," Bill yelled. "We took thet tater off and the hair was gone."

"Bill, I already dun told ya," said Skeeter. "White hairs gonna grow in there now. He'll be disguised."

Now I couldn't see his face, but the way the Major's back straightened quickly, I don't think he was too pleased at this development.

"A bald spot on his forehead is not going to increase his value, Mr. Shafer, but I will pay you something for your time."

Shafer smiled at him. It was a wide-toothy grin, but not necessarily friendly.

"Well, I heard you say you were going to sell that horse for five hundred dollars. I never had me a five-hundred-dollar horse here before. The price is gonna go up considerable."

The Major stiffened at this comment. He stared at Shafer for a moment before turning in the saddle and opening up the saddlebag on his left-hand side. He rummaged around inside for a moment and pulled out a coin.

"Here is a twenty-dollar gold piece. That is more than fair."

He tossed it towards Shafer who snatched it out of the air with his right hand. "A lot more where that came from?" he asked.

With that, the Major reached down with his right hand and undid the clasp on the holster of his sidearm. The woman noticed this and raised the muzzle of the shotgun towards him again. Mike Shafer walked towards his wife, shaking his head like he was about to scold a child.

"Careful with that shotgun, dear," said Mike, a tone of concern in his voice. "No need for anyone to get hurt. We are just negotiating a price."

He pushed the barrels of the shotgun skyward. When it was pointed harmlessly at the heavens, he ripped the double-barreled shotgun out of his wife's hands and in one smooth motion whirled around, catching the rebel officer off guard.

KA-BOOM

The Major was able to get his revolver out of its holster, but the shotgun blast hit him in the chest and knocked him off the back of his horse. The refined Southern gentleman flopped on the ground like a bag of dirty laundry and his horse and the two horses he was holding went into a panic from the shotgun blast.

Bill had drawn his pistol when he saw Mike fire the shotgun, but the frantic horses soon blocked his view. The Major's horse, his ear bleeding from stray shotgun pellets, pushed by him and nearly knocked him over. Before Bill could recover his balance, Shafer fired the second barrel and caught Bill in the midsection. It knocked him backwards and he sprawled in pain in the middle of the barnyard.

Skeeter was holding onto the reins of Trooper, but the big horse was pulling away. The gimpy reb was half turned around when he saw Bill fall, and he dropped the reins and went for his gun. Shafer tossed away the empty shotgun and dove to the ground to recover the Major's pistol. Skeeter got off two shots, but they kicked up dust on either side of Shafer. Eli was right. He had said Skeeter was too nervous to be a marksman under pressure. Mike Shafer steadied his aim from a prone position and fired three well-placed shots. Two of the three hit Skeeter in the chest and he crumpled to the ground. We could hear him gasping for breath as the blood filled his lungs. Then he was still except for his good leg that was twitching with some sort of death spasms.

I started gasping for breath too. In less time than it took me to tie my shoes, I had seen three men die violently. I had never seen a dead person before until last fall when my mother insisted I attend the wake of an elderly neighbor. Now three men lie dead just a stone's throw away from me, their bodies oozing blood onto the dusty ground of the barnyard.

"Ben, you gotta be quiet. He'll hear ya," whispered Eli putting his hand over my mouth. "You're as white as a ghost. Are you alright?"

I looked up at him in a daze. Gray Wolf was crouched down and hovering protectively over us. Then Eli got a strange look on his face and pulled away. He half-ran, half-crawled about thirty feet towards where the horses were tied up and began to throw up.

I was definitely not all right, and either was Eli. Gray Wolf laid down beside me and patted me on the shoulder for reassurance.

He had undoubtedly witnessed many violent deaths in his lifetime, some at his own hands. We watched as Eli wiped his mouth on his sleeve. He shrugged his shoulders to tell us it was nothing. He always felt the need to be the tough one—my big brother.

Mike Shafer stood in the middle of the barnyard that was now suddenly silent. Gray Wolf slipped back to where the horses were tied to calm them. A telltale whinny from any one of them would be heard in this quiet after the storm. It would certainly be our death knell.

"Don't stand there, woman," Shafer shouted at his wife. "Help me round up these horses."

She was standing there as though frozen in place. If the stories were true, Shafer had killed dozens of men, but she had probably never witnessed his grim work before. I tried not to even think of the rumor that he had killed his younger daughter for talking to a posse. He would definitely have no problem killing two boys and an old Indian.

"Get moving, you old witch, before I give you a kick in the backside."

This forced her into action. She rounded the side of the cabin in search of the horse that had disappeared around the corner.

Mike walked slowly to the horse Skeeter had been riding and gathered in its reins. The Major's horse had taken off at a gallop down the road. We saw it as it passed close to us, it's eyes wild with excitement. Its right ear was torn off by the shotgun blast and its blood mingled with the Major's blood on the saddle. Trooper was trying to pull backwards from Skeeter when everything happened. When Skeeter released him, the big stallion backed into the corral and stayed in the far corner.

Holding the reins of the horse, Shafer picked up Skeeter's body with his right hand and threw it across the saddle. Then he moved over to Bill's body, which was considerably heavier. He stepped on the dangling reins with his left foot to hold the frightened animal in place. With both hands now free, he lifted Bill's body and put it behind the saddle.

"We'll put that reb Major on that one," said Shafer to his wife as she brought Bill's horse to him. "We gotta make these bodies disappear in the black bog in case somebody heard all that ruckus and sends another posse out here. Too much damn law around here nowadays."

The Major's bloody corpse was the closest to us and as Shafer pulled it up to put it on the horse, he turned and looked our way. Having the killer cast his eyes in our direction made my blood run cold. *Did he hear us*? Fear like I have never felt before seized my body. If he was coming for us, I am sure I could not move. But instead he turned back towards his task, tossing the Major's body onto the horse.

When he was done, Shafer's shirt was drenched red with blood. The scatter gun's blast had caught the Major in the upper chest and neck and blood had poured forth like a dam bursting.

Shafer began leading the horse to the trail that led to the Black Marsh. He motioned for his wife to follow with the horse that he had stacked the bodies of Skeeter and Bill on. Then he turned suddenly as if something had just occurred to him.

"Birdie, get out here girl," he yelled towards the cabin. "I got something for you to do."

After a few long moments, a shy-looking girl appeared in the doorway. She was about Eli's age, maybe fourteen or fifteen, and not unpleasant to look upon. She seemed petrified with fear.

"Birdie, get down the road and fetch that reb Major's horse. It's covered in blood and if it runs towards the village, the law will be coming around asking questions. They got themselves a Justice of the Peace now. Getting too civilized around here. When I came here some thirty years ago, nobody questioned a man about his business."

It seemed a might strange to hear this killer lamenting about the coming of civilization, but I guess you had to look at it from his viewpoint. What he said was not entirely true. Although they were a vigilante group, the Jasper County Rangers in the earlier days kept the outlaws of the swamp country in check.

And who can forget Mr. Hess capturing Mike Shafer and sending him to prison for a few years. Old Shaf never forgot, that's for sure. He had killed, butchered or stole over fifty head of horses from Momence's leading citizen in the years since.

Birdie, as she was called, gave her father a wide berth as she went around him and headed down the road towards Lake Village to retrieve the blood-soaked horse. She passed close by us and we all held our breath. We were hoping the horses would not make a noise that would put her on to our hiding place among the oak scrub and weeds. Shafer and his wife gradually disappeared down a pathway to the Black Marsh leading the horses that carried their sad burden. *The barnyard was suddenly empty.*

I felt Gray Wolf nudge me forward, but I didn't need any prodding to know this was our opportunity. We got up and moved stealthily across the barnyard towards the corral where Trooper had come to a halt at the far end.

We split up and approached the big stallion from either side. He looked at me and then at Eli and, as much as a horse shows recognition, accepted that we were there for him. Skeeter and Bill had already put a bridle on him so that helped. I thought we might need Maggie to lead him out after the stress he had just been through, but it was not necessary; he came along willingly.

That was fortunate since Gray Wolf had already taken the other horses up the road. When we caught up with him, Gray Wolf was attempting to mount the mare, but his efforts fell short. He slid down her side to the ground. Eli clasped his hands together and bracing himself making a stirrup for the old warrior to step into. This time he accepted Eli's help, and he was able to get his right leg over the back of the mare. As reluctant as he was to being helped, he apparently realized that it was no time to be proud. *We had to get out of here fast!*

~

CHAPTER 21
A Chance Encounter

After we were all mounted up and ready to go, Eli turned the dappled filly he was riding towards the barnyard once more.

"We'll leave that gate open just like we found it," he said. "Shafer will think Trooper just wandered off. He won't 'spect somebody took'em."

"Okay," I said. "I'll believe it if you will."

It was true we caught a lucky break when Shafer forgot to close the corral gate after all the excitement. Hopefully he would blame the absence of Trooper on his own negligence and not search the maze of footprints and hoofprints in the barnyard for another explanation.

Since I was on a gelding and had a saddle with a nice saddle horn, Eli thought it best I trail Trooper behind me. He didn't want the stallion getting frisky; we had no time for that. He and Gray Wolf rode behind me on the filly and the mare.

After travelling a half mile west into the failing light of sunset, we got a surprise. Not a pleasant one, mind you. Birdie emerged from the narrow path through the scrub oak that we had passed earlier. She had her back to me as she tugged on the reins of the Major's runaway horse. I stopped in the middle of the trail, and she almost backed into me. When she realized I was there, she jumped back, startled. I said nothing—I had no idea what to say. Then her brow began to furrow, and she looked at me suspiciously.

"That big horse you're leading was in my father's corral. Did you take him outah there?"

"Well," I said after a moment of hesitation. "He's mine."

"Oh," she answered after thinking that over. "Well, I knew he was somebody's. Sure didn't belong to those rebs who showed up for him. I knew they stole him." Then she got a funny look on her face and cast her eyes downward, not saying anymore. She was probably wondering if she had said too much. She may have been wondering what we had seen already and what we already knew.

"My name is Ben...ah, Tyler." I knew giving my own name wouldn't be wise. Eli was on Mr. Tyler's filly and his was the first name to come to mind.

"We're from Morocco," said Eli. He had dismounted and was by my side, glancing up nervously, afraid I would say the wrong thing. I could assure him I was not going to give Mike Shafer's daughter any information he could use to find us.

"If you're going back to Morocco, you best be takin' that trail I just come offah. It goes in a straight line right to the lake. It's the way my Daddy goes."

Yeah, I thought, *a straight line to Bogus Island where he can pick up some more stolen horses.*

"Thank you kindly fer pointing that out, missy," said Eli in his politest voice.

"My Daddy calls me Birdie," she offered. "Says that cause he swears he's gonna have to clip my wings someday."

She did not say this in jest. Her face turned sour as green apples when the words came out of her mouth. I looked at Eli and he looked at me. *Was he thinking what I was thinking*? Was Birdie's little shudder because she was thinking of what happened to her younger sister?

"Okay, thanks for your advice," I said. "We have to be going now. The sun has almost set, and the mosquitoes are going to eat us alive."

She stood there waiting for us to make the first move. We sure didn't want to take her advice and descend into a trail going south through the Black Marsh. That was not the direction we wanted to go. Mr. Trowbridge's quote from Sir Walter Scott flashed through my mind: "Oh, what a tangled web we weave, when first we practice to deceive."

"Yeah, those flyin' bloodsuckers are bad here," said Eli, breaking the silence. "Some real gallnappers. You best be gettin' home too."

Birdie turned and tugged on the reins of the Major's horse. We did not move as we waited for her to round the bend before riding on.

"Ya'll aren't going to Morocco, are ya?" she asked, turning around once more to face us. "That nervous little fella with the gimpy leg talked too much. He said they stole that big stallion outah a stable in Momence. Said they got a spotter there that finds'um good horses."

Whoa! Now what do we do? We had been caught flat-footed in a lie. I looked down at Eli who was still standing by the side of my horse. He was older and was the quickest thinker when it came to tight situations.

He looked up at me and gave me a sheepish grin. *That's all you got?* I thought.

"Are you gonna tell your father?" I asked. *Might as well get it out there.*

"Naw, I don't tell that man nothin' I don't have to. He's an evil man, low as pond scum. I'm ashamed to say I sprung from his loins."

"Birdie, you don't have ta go back there if'un ya don't wantah," said Eli.

Whoa! What are we supposed to do with her? I felt sorry for her, but who in Momence is going to want to take in Mike Shafer's daughter. Everybody in town knows the terrible price Mr. Hess paid for crossing Old Shaf. I guess we could put her in our spare bedroom unless Frank has talked his way in there since I've been gone.

"Thank you," she said to Eli sincerely, wiping the telltale tear from her cheek. "I couldn't do that and leave my mother alone in that house with him."

"Sometimes ya just gotta take care of yourself."

Her care-worn face softened up a bit and she gave Eli a hint of a smile.

"What's your name?"

"Eli."

"Thank you, Eli, but the time's not right now. Something bad just happened and I gotta stay with my mom. I'll get away from him someday. I'll go someplace he can't find me."

With this she turned and led the Major's horse with the bloody saddle down the road.

~

CHAPTER 22
Night Falls

Gray Wolf and I had travelled a ways up the road before Eli caught up with us. He had been watching Birdie walk back towards the Shafer cabin until she rounded the bend and was out of sight. Birdie wasn't bad to look at, so maybe that was it. Eli is a couple years older than me and is of the age he is thinking about girls. I have had some strange, fleeting thoughts about them that I do not completely understand, and I've been told it's only going to get worse.

On the other hand, it could be Eli's protective streak. He feels like he has to take care of everyone around him. So, it could be his sense of responsibility or maybe just "puppy love" — I don't know which, but Eli and Birdie shared a moment back there. It could be that both are outsiders. Maybe that was their connection. They were both a notch or two away from proper society.

I know a little about how that feels. Before the war, my dad and Libby's dad, Major Carter, were what people referred to as "leading citizens". The stable was doing well, and we had some land outside of town. We were well off by Momence standards, I suppose. After my father didn't come home from the war, the stable couldn't produce a decent profit no matter how hard Eli and I tried. Folks didn't have much confidence in a couple of kids.

Now Libby's family remained a part of proper society because, even though her father took to drinking after the war, he did it in private. Her grandfather ran things in the family business, and they were doing well. Mrs. Carter and my mother had been the best of friends, always planning parties and social events. Some were for a good purpose like the Widows and Orphans Fund; my mother never imagined herself being a recipient.

Now as for Libby and me, we still remained the best of friends because we grew up together. It didn't matter to her that the Tanners had slipped few rungs down the social ladder. Kids don't pay too much attention to that stuff. It nearly killed my mother though. Not having the leisure time or money to remain part of that social circle sent her into a sad state of mind. Sure, Mrs. Carter talked to her if they met on the street, but it just wasn't the same.

"We gotta find a place to put up for the night," Eli announced as he pulled up between Gray Wolf and me. He turned towards the old warrior for guidance on this particular problem.

"We find fish shack of man we pass on river. It was close. Not good for two boys from town to spend night in swamp."

Eli's lip curled up at the "town boys" remark, but he said nothing. He knew without Gray Wolf we would be completely lost in this vast wilderness. I am sure Gray Wolf meant no insult by the remark. That was not part of his nature.

Staying in the fishing shack would be a problem if Mr. Bunch was still there. He would have more questions than I cared to answer. I would rather sleep in the marsh, truth be told.

When we reached the river, it was in the moonlight. We did not cross it but followed the riverbank until we came to the bayou where Bunch's fishing shack was located. There was no light inside, so he must have gone back to Lake Village rather than stay the night on the river. Without the moonlight, we would have had a difficult time tying up the horses for the night. With that done, we entered the fish shack. The door was not locked or barred in any way. Since the builders do not own the wilderness land they are built upon, fish shacks were not viewed as a home but more or less common property. Most men who built one of these crude structures didn't mind if travelers stayed there overnight. I hoped Mr. Bunch was such a man.

There was a crude table and chairs inside in front of a fireplace. The last occupant had left a few logs and Eli favored making a fire. I didn't like the idea. If Birdie told her father, we might have Old Shaf tracking us at night. The cheery glow of a fire inside the fish shack would certainly give us away.

"No fire," said Gray Wolf, ending the discussion.

There were burlap grain sacks to roll down and cover the four open windows. I hoped that would help keep the mosquitoes out. In one corner there were two straw beds that Gray Wolf insisted we take since he preferred sleeping sitting upright. As I laid in the still darkness, the savagery of what we had witnessed at Shafer's cabin began to settle into my mind.

"Hey," I whispered to Eli.

"What?"

"Those men getting killed back there. I know they were thieves and worst of all, rebs, but that was a terrible way to go."

"Yeah, I wish ya didn't have ta see that. It was pretty terrible."

It was terrible for both of us, I thought to myself. I remembered Eli slipping back towards the horses and throwing up. Sometimes it irritates me that he always thinks of himself as a grown up and me as a kid; we are only two years apart.

Maybe he was just being the man he thought he had to be. His grandpappy was very close to my father and took over the running of the stable after my father left for the war. After his stroke, he could not work or even talk. So maybe Eli felt he had two households to take care of. Eli never shirked from responsibility.

"I was thinking of my dime novel *The Mysterious Major, Was He Blue or Was He Gray*. It was part of Beadles Civil War editions."

"You back ta thinkin' 'bout that book again? What about it?"

"The drawing on the cover was just as he was getting shot and it looked kind of exciting. You know, like dying in battle—you know, like courageous and brave and all."

171

"Well, there ain't nothin' courageous or brave 'bout dying like that. It's just messy."

"Poor Skeeter, he was gasping for breath after Shafer shot him in the chest. Don't think I'll ever forget that gurgling sound he made."

"Poor Skeeter woulda put ah bullet in ya without givin' it ah thought if'en he caught us takin' those hosses back. You best forget about all that and get some sleep. We're gonna have a big day tomorrow."

With this, he rolled over and turned his back to me. I wondered, if we ever made it home, if we would ever speak of this again.

~

CHAPTER 23
Sudden Danger

Gray Wolf woke us as the first light of dawn began to seep through the burlap curtains. Eli and I were up and outside with the horses quick as could be. I sure wished we had some of those corn dodgers left because I was mighty hungry. No time to think about food though.

Old Shaf could be on our trail. Gray Wolf found a stump so he did not have to rely on Eli to help him onboard Maggie. I had left the gelding saddled all night and I checked the cinch strap to make sure it was still tight. When I was mounted up, Eli gave me the lead rope to Trooper before he sprang onto the back of the dappled-gray filly.

We had to back track a ways to get back to the river ford we had crossed the previous evening and I didn't like going back in the direction of Shafer's cabin. I had this picture in my mind of us running head on into the killer as he was pursuing us. Eli assured me that Birdie wouldn't tell Shafer that she saw us with the black stallion. I did not share his confidence.

When we crossed the ford to the north side of the river and were heading west back towards Illinois again, I felt relieved. Even if Birdie didn't put him onto us, Mike Shafer might be a great tracker and, who knows, he might be able to figure out from the scrambled mess of hoofprints and footprints in the barn yard that Trooper didn't wander out of the corral on his own.

Eli said I was fretting way too much. I think maybe if you really fear somebody, you imagine they have all sorts of powers and abilities they don't necessarily possess. I hoped that was the case with me.

Gray Wolf was in the lead. When he got to an open clearing along the river, he turned suddenly, raising his hand for us to stop. Before I could ask why, there was a low, thundering sound and the ground started shaking. I dismounted and stood on the trembling earth with the reins of the gelding in one hand and the lead rope to Trooper in the other. That is when the source of the disturbance appeared.

"Yanasi," said Gray Wolf.

"Buffalo," said Eli.

They dashed headlong into the river with no hesitation—bulls, cows and an even a few calves. There were couple hundred in all.

"Yep, they can swim too," said Eli with his little snicker of a laugh.

"Hey, I didn't ask, did I?"

"I figured you were 'bout to."

Since we could not go any further until they passed, Eli and Gray Wolf seemed content to sit and watch. I watched too, but with one eye looking over my shoulder for Old Shaf. The bulls were larger and in the lead. It was a lot like watching a bunch of young men at a town dance.

The biggest bulls were pushing against the smaller ones and tossed around their horns in a threatening manner, showing them who was boss. The cows were more docile and seemed to be very protective of the calves.

"Herd small now," Gray Wolf observed sadly when they had finally passed. It was true that buffalo hunters had taken their toll on the herd. Tons of bison meat was shipped to Chicago to feed the growing population of the city by the lake.

The herd might get a break now since a lot of the buffalo hunters have gone west to supply the workers on the transcontinental railroad. I read in the newspaper the buffalo herds on the plains were huge—more than a man could count. What's left of the little herd here in the marsh might be wiped out someday, but there aren't enough bullets to wipe out the great herds on the plains. The newspaper estimated there were millions of buffalo out west.

Gray Wolf made a clucking sound that signaled Maggie it was time to move. We followed him over the trampled ground on the riverbank where the herd had passed. There were two fishermen in a crude, home-made boat who had pulled over to the opposite shore when they heard the buffalo coming.

They looked at us curiously and waved, but we did not stop to talk. We had no time for idle conversation. Mike Shafer might be on our trail right now. We had to keep moving.

In less than an hour we were in sight of Dr. Shronts's cabin. Eli was quick to notice that Scarlett, the red pony, was not tied to the tree as we had left her. She had a big appetite for a little horse so the doctor may have moved her to a greener pasture. We dismounted and stretched our legs and backs; they were stiff from our time in the saddle.

Me and Eli approached the cabin, jumping up on the low porch. I was about to knock when the bullet hit the door.

"*Bam*!"

~

CHAPTER 24
The Missing Rider

"I'm sorry fellers," gushed Sam Patch. "I been nervous as ah long-tailed cat in ah room full ah rockin' chairs." He was limping around on a homemade crutch.

"No harm done," I assured him. "The door is so thick it stopped the bullet."

Of course, if the bullet had hit one of the cracks in the rough-hewn door, it would have come through and killed me.

"You need ta look a'fore ya shoot next time," Eli pointed out.

"Doc give me laudanum fer the pain and it made me a little crazy. When I heard ya'll out there on the porch, I thought sure Gib come back da do me in."

"Gib?" I looked at Eli. "Wasn't he the tracker that disappeared from the Major's party?"

Eli turned to Sam. "Didn't you say that was the feller wearin' the coonskin cap yesterday?"

"Yep, thet be him. He stole thet red pony back fer the Major. Dr. Shronts heared him out there and hollered at'em. The Doc ducked back in here ta get his shotgun, but Gib was down the road a'fore he could get a shot off."

"Where is Doctor Shronts now?" I asked.

"He went into town ta get the Justice of the Peace. Don't know what he could do to catch ole Gib? He's slippery as ah greased snake. I guess the Doc jest wanted ta report the theft, thet bein' the proper thing ta do."

Then something else caught my attention. It was the smell of food. Except for the rabbit we all shared at Gray Wolf's camp, we had been eating nothing but corn dodgers and stale bread. Sam saw me staring at the table where his dish remained half full. We had interrupted his morning meal.

"You fellers want somethin' ta eat?"

"We sure do!" I was the first to jump at the offer.

Eli walked over to the table and looked in the pot.

"Rabbit stew?"

"Oh, we had rabbit yesterday," I said. "I'll have some anyhow."

"Well, fellers, I've et lots ah rabbit but never like this. Doc made it a'fore he left. It's German rabbit stew. It's got mushrooms, carrots and all kinds of good stuff in it. He even poured in ah glass of wine fer good measure. Best I ever tasted."

I spooned up a bowl full and dug in. It was an experience, all right. Usually I just ate to fill my belly, but this dish had my lips smacking together in appreciation. Eli, of course, being Eli, had to poke around in it awhile with that skeptical look on his face. I guess that was part of his need to always be in control. It took him awhile to get enthused about anything anybody else suggested.

We were so happy to have a good meal, we forgot about Gray Wolf. He was still standing by the door looking out warily for anyone that might want to do us harm.

"Gray Wolf. Come over here and have some of this rabbit stew," I insisted.

The old warrior looked at me without smiling and turned back to check once more for enemies before coming over to the table. I gave him a steaming bowlful and he looked at it without enthusiasm before putting a spoonful in his mouth. His stone face began to melt into a smile as the flavor captured him.

"Rabbit?" he questioned.

"Yeah, and a bunch of other good stuff," I said.

"Come on and sit down." Eli invited, slapping the bench next to him.

Gray Wolf cautiously sat down and finished the bowl of stew. Then lifted his bowl towards me.

"More." It came out more of a demand than a request.

As I dished the last of the delicious German rabbit stew into the old warrior's bowl, Eli and Sam started laughing. I began laughing too at the way he said it. Gray Wolf sure took a fancy to Doctor Shronts's stew. It was good to laugh again after the three days we had endured.

We had a carefree moment before Gray Wolf turned his attention to the open door again. *Who's out there?* It could be Gib after the other horses or it could be worse—Old Shaf, after revenge. Sam Patch's smile faded as a grim realization hit him.

"I wonder if Gib knows I'm here?"

"Did he see you when he stole the red pony?"

"Naw, just Doctor Shronts. I was still lyin' on the table gettin' used to my leg splint. I knew who it was when Doc said he were wearin' a coonskin hat."

"Did he shoot at Doctor Shronts?" I asked.

"Naw, he knows better then ta do thet. If'en he kilt the Doc, every man in Lake Village would be out lookin' fer'em. I never did live in ah town lucky enough ta have ah doctor. I never see'd ah doctor 'cept when I was in the army. They were army surgeons thet cut off arms and legs. They're not like real doctors thet could cure ah body of somethin'."

"Well," I said, "the best thing we can do for Doctor Shronts is to high tail it out of here before we bring Mike Shafer down on him. He's going to come looking for Trooper."

"I don't believe Birdie's gonna tell him squat," said Eli.

"I don't have no fear of this Mike Shafer," said Sam. "He's got no reason ta come after me. I'm worried 'bout Gib comin' back. If he figur's out from tracks and all that I'm here, he'll tell the Major and they'll all be over ta finish me. The Major never did get his head outah the military. He considers me ah deserter and he will want ta have me shot."

Eli and I looked at each other, deciding which one of us would break the news to him, when Gray Wolf spoke up.

"All dead," he said bluntly with a wave of his hand as though he was sweeping them off the table.

"What?"

"It's true," I assured him. "We saw it. It was terrible. They are all dead."

"But how?"

"Old Shaf," said Eli. "Never seen anythin' like it. He gunned them all down in the blink of an eye."

"The Major, Skeeter and Bill?"

"Ever mother's son of'um," said Eli.

Sam Patch sat there looking at his hands for a moment letting it all sink in.

"I guess I should be glad but somehow I don't feel that way. I left cuz I was tired of runnin' and thievin', but they were my comrades fer awhile. The Major got me outah Tennessee. If'en I stayed there, I would been dead fer sure by now."

"Well, you just have to get that out of your mind," I said. "They would have done you harm for sure. You don't have to worry about them anymore."

"Do ya think Gib knows? He'll probably just ride off if he finds out the Majors dead."

"Doubt it," said Eli. "Old Shaf done away with those bodies right quick."

"Then there's the Sarge," said Sam. "I suppose somebody outah tell him. He'll probably just go back to Alabama."

"Who's the Sarge?" I asked.

"He's the one spots all the good horse for'em. Got himself a job workin' in a stable in Momence. He gets to see the best horse flesh in town."

My stomach churned when I heard this. It felt like it was going to come up in my throat and choke me.

"What's the Sarge's real name?" asked Eli slowly.

"Why I believe it's Frank. Yeah, that's it. Frank."

~

CHAPTER 25
A Sad Parting

"**M**r. Frank don't sound like no Johnny reb," said Eli.

"He was a guard at Andersonville," Sam pointed out. "He learned ta talk like ah Yankee from listening ta the prisoners."

"My father's letters!"

"What about'em?" asked Eli.

"That's where he learned all about our family so he could pretend he served under my father and was his friend."

"The Sarge is ah first rate con man," said Sam. "Ain't no doubt about that."

"We got to go now," I announced suddenly. As what Sam had revealed to us sank in, I was on the verge of panic. My mother was by herself in the presence of a Confederate criminal. Though, according to Sam Patch, the gang did not consider themselves criminals—they were still soldiers fighting an endless war.

I got up from the table and ran through the door out onto the porch. I stopped when I realized I had no idea what to do first. We could take the canoe. It was laying in the grass just off the edge of the porch. It was mid-morning. If we took it, going down-stream now, we could easily travel the fourteen or so miles to Momence before sunset. That would mean leaving Trooper, Maggie and Mr. Tyler's filly. With Gib lurking around, that wasn't a good option. He had already snatched Libby's red pony.

Eli was looking at me, sensing my mind had scattered.

"Ben, you get on the filly and I'll ride Trooper and let's go."

"What about Maggie?"

Eli's face screwed up like he had thought of something that was difficult to say.

"Ben, how much ya think that old mare's worth? She's nigh onto twenty years old and she's a might sway back and getting' kinda spavin."

It occurred to me where all this was going. "You want to give Maggie to Gray Wolf?"

"Well, now that ya mentioned it, that's a great idea!"

"The old warrior does seem to be quite fond of her."

"That's not exactly how I would put it, but we're thinkin' along the same lines. This here mission, as you like ta call it, would have been doomed from the get go if'un he hadn't come along. Givin' Gray Wolf that old horse would make his day."

"I suppose Maggie is only worth twenty dollars or so."

"If that."

Eli took that as agreement and turned to Sam Patch who was standing on the porch leaning on his crutch.

"Sam, we're leavin' the sorrel mare fer Gray Wolf. Ya better let him take yer gelding away from here and hide him. Gib might come back here and try to steal'em."

"Yeah, and he might 'cide ta do me in long as he's here. I ain't no match fer him hobblin' round with this splint on my leg."

"What about Libby's canoe?" I asked.

"We can't make any time draggin' a canoe behind us. It's safe here at the Doc's."

"Gib ain't gonna steal no canoe," Sam assured me. "He's ah horse thief."

Now it was time to say good-bye to Gray Wolf, our guide through the outlaw country. I should say protector too. He sure was that. We would have never got our horses off Bogus Island without him. I wanted to run up and give the old warrior a hug, but I followed Eli's lead and gave the respectful hand sign. I raised my right hand, palm out, and waved with my fingers.

"We will miss you, Gray Wolf," I said.

"Not for long," he replied with a slight smile. "You must come back for canoe."

Eli and I both got a laugh out of that.

"We'll try ta get back fer it by the next full moon," Eli said.

I don't know if that was going to be possible. If we make it back from this adventure, the adults might be watching us real close. Slipping away to the marsh lands of Indiana might be tougher the next time. Libby would tell me to forget about the canoe. Another trip into outlaw country was not worth it.

I knew I would return to this wild country some day in spite of the outlaws that used it as their haven. I had never been to a place so full of life as the marsh. As I was standing, looking west, a flight of pure white swans passed overhead and landed in the river. The skies were filled with geese, wood ducks, teal and about any other kind of bird a guy could think of. We scarcely travelled a mile without seeing a fox, deer, muskrat or beaver. I knew I would return, and often.

"Ben, come on. Quit standing around daydreaming. We're burnin' daylight." Eli was halfway to the river before I caught up.

~

CHAPTER 26
Headed Home

Eli and I started on the trail back to Momence at a gallop which soon slowed to a trot and eventually a walk. The bank along the river became thicker and thicker with water willows and reeds that stood above our heads. We dismounted and led the horses away from the river through thickets of saw grass and scrub oak.

We were especially wary of the black bogs that Sam Patch warned us about. They were ponds that after many years became covered with leaves and branches until they looked like ground that you could walk on. You couldn't. Sam said they were the final resting place for outlaws who died or any other body a desperado wished to get rid of. I thought of Mike Shafer slipping the bodies of Skeeter, Bill and the Major into one.

Then an unlikely obstruction barred our way. We came upon two sand hill cranes with a nest close to the riverbank. They were hovering around two eggs that were sitting in a large nest made of twigs and reed stems. As we stepped into the clearing, the proud daddy came after us. The big gray bird was very upset at our being there. He rushed at us flapping his wings and pecking at us with his long, sharp beak. He was about four-foot-tall, but when he flapped his wings, he looked to be seven foot wide. We fled the area pulling the horses behind us. Trooper's eyes were open wide with excitement and his nostrils flared. He wanted nothing to do with the huge angry bird.

"We gotta cross the river," said Eli, pointing to the opposite bank. There was a wide sand beach with no overgrowth or plants to slow us down. If we could get the horses across, we could make good time. The sun was already high overhead, and we didn't know what other obstacles we were going to encounter.

Eli rode Trooper to the river and the big stallion balked. There was a steep bank to negotiate. It was not high, only about three feet, but the water below was covered with duckweed and other water plants. A horse will not move if it is unsure of its footing. I know the little filly I was riding was waiting to see what Trooper did.

Eli slid off Trooper's back and pushed the weeds aside to enter the water. When he did, he disappeared for a moment. The high bank should have told us this was the natural course of the river, and we would be entering deep water.

"We better go back to where we crossed the other day," I said. "Back by where the ditch came out."

Eli moved away from the bank and had to tread water. He came back to the bank and started pushing the duckweed out of the way.

"We do that," he said, looking up at the sun, "we're gonna lose too much time."

He scrambled up the steep bank and took Trooper's reins. With soothing words of encouragement, Eli eased the big stallion into the water. I could see the panic in the horse's eyes when he could not find footing, but Eli swam ahead, pulling on the lead rope as he did. After swimming about thirty feet, both Eli and Trooper found footing at the bottom of the river. When they reached the opposite shore, he motioned for me to follow.

Well, that looked easy enough, I thought. I knew it wasn't. Slipping off the back of the filly, I pulled her towards the riverbank. Her nostrils were flared, and she was nervous. She definitely wanted to follow Trooper; her herding instinct was kicking in.

I slid down the bank into the water with the reins in my hand. The filly pulled her head back and pawed the edge of the bank before finally coming into the water. I swam ahead of her, pulling her along. The filly was wild-eyed until we reached the shallow water and she could walk out.

Me and Eli sat side-by-side in the sand for a moment looking at the opposite shore.

"We did it," I said.

"Ya didn't think we could, did ya?" Eli gave me a punch in the arm.

We got up and were brushing the sand off our pants when a voice came out of no-where.

"Good job, boys. Ya'll gottem across the river. I'da had some trouble get'em across myself."

We both turned around slowly and saw the intruder. He was a thin man with a red-dish-colored beard that was stained with dark streaks from chewing tobacco that fell short of its mark. He wore a sinister grin and a coonskin cap.

"Gib," I said without thinking.

~

CHAPTER 27
Taken Hostage

Gib raised his pistol and pointed it to the east. "I thought you boys woulda crossed the river at that ford down by the ditch. I had ta hide my hoss in the bushes and follower ya'll on foot. Now we gotta go back'n get'em."

"Go ahead," said Eli. "We'll wait fer ya."

Again, the sinister smile. "Yer ah smart-mouth young'en. I cun take thet sass outah ya."

I motioned with my hand for Eli to back down. We had come through so much in the last few days. We were just a half day's ride from home. Now this reb scout was going to take the horses back. The big question: *What was he going to do with us?* I didn't have to wait long for the answer to that.

"I'm gonna take you two smart asses back to the Major and see what he wants ta do with ya. I hopes he says ta string ya up by yer thumbs and leave ya fer the buzzards." With this, he motioned with his head to the sky where a half-dozen vultures were flying in a lazy loop over on the other side of the river. With all the life that was abound in the marsh, there was, of course, always death.

"Gib, the Major is dead." I saw no reason to try to soften the blow for the misguided reb who was still bent on fighting for a defeated cause. "We saw him die."

Gib looked at me in total disbelief. He looked stunned. *This wasn't going to be easy.*

"That's right," Eli assured him. "We saw Mike Shafer gun him down along with Bill and Skeeter."

"Naw, I don't believe you two little Yanks."

"We saw Shafer cart the bodies off to sink them in a bog." I thought the more details we could give him, the more we could convince him that what we were telling him was true.

"Yeah, the Major captured us and was gonna kill us, but Mike Shafer came along and saved us. We're friends of Old Shaf."

Wow, Eli had just come up with a whopper. I felt a need to jump in and do my part.

"Yeah, anything bad happens to us, you're going to have to answer to Mike Shafer."

We shut up and let this sink in to Gib's slow moving brain. His eyes squinted as he tried to digest all this. Unfortunately, in the end, the sinister smile returned.

"I don't believe none of thet story. No backwoods outlaw gonna outshoot the Major with Bill and Skeeter at his side. Them boys were at Chickamauga. They was in the battle ah Lookout Mountain fightin' hand ta hand up there in the clouds. Ain't no way one man stood agin'em."

"If'en it ain't true, how do we know yer name is Gib."

"Yeah," I chimed in. "How would we know that if we weren't captured by the Major? We have never met you before."

Again, the squinty eyes as he considered this new piece of information. We didn't see the confident, sinister smile but we still hadn't totally convinced him.

"Grab those hosses's reins," he announced. "We gotta walk a bit ta get my hoss."

Gib started marching us back up the river with the horses in tow. Gib stayed out front for a short ways, but got tired of turning around to watch us and moved to the side of Trooper, still waving his gun around menacingly. We were walking along a sand ridge with water on either side. It looked very familiar. It was the dune where we had stopped to have lunch the first day out.

"You suppose he's really going to shoot us?" I whispered to Eli.

"Depends on how much ah that Mike Shafer yarn he believes. Nobody crosses Old Shaf out here in the swamp. Ah course, maybe Gib ain't been around here long 'nough ta know that."

"Hey, you two," shouted Gib as he moved to the front of the horses again. "Shut yer pie-holes. I don't want no talkin' up here."

"Okay Gib," said Eli. "We'll be quiet as church mice."

After walking a few paces with us, his curiosity got the better of him.

"How would ah couple ah young'en the likes of yuse fellers know Mike Shafer?"

The bobber just went down. Fish on!

"My father does business with Mike." It was my turn to tell a whopper. "We help. We find quality horses in town for him to steal."

"Oh, yer spotters. Just like Frank."

Yeah, just like Frank. My teeth were grinding after that assessment. I thought of my mother alone with that deceitful reb hanging around. It appeared that Gib had swallowed enough of our story to make him think twice about gunning us down. We had to get back to Momence and pronto. It was time to try something desperate.

~

CHAPTER 28
A Familiar Spot

Eli and I had to think of something quick. We were going backwards, away from Momence, walking on top a sandbar with the river to our left and stagnant water to our right. We tugged the reins of the horses as we pulled them along while Gib walked beside us waving his pistol around. After about a hundred yards, he got tired and dropped back a little. Eli took the opportunity to tug on my shirt sleeve and whisper his plan.

"See that branch laying there up ahead. You remember this spot?"

"It seems kinda familiar."

"When we get to that branch, I'm pushin' Trooper ta the right. When I do, let go that filly and foller me. We're gonna run like hell."

I nodded in agreement, terrified as to what was about to happen. How were we going to outrun a bullet if Gib's first reaction was to shoot us?

Suddenly Eli whirled around and threw Trooper's reins up in the air. "Yaw" he shouted, while waving his arms around wildly. The big stallion was startled and jumped sideways knocking Gib down the side of the sand dune. I followed Eli as he ran full-tilt for about twenty yards and then suddenly veered off at a right angle and ran down the side of the sand dune. When we reached the stagnant water, Gib fired a warning shot. It was well over our heads, but it froze Eli in place. He raised his hands in surrender and I did likewise, just following his lead.

This seemed to please Gib and I could see his sinister little grin from thirty yards away.

"Ya'll get back har ya little Yankee brats."

Eli began to back up, still keeping his hands raised.

"I don't think our parents would approve of us goin' with you, sir."

What was Eli doing? He sounded like a whippy little schoolboy, but he continued to back up. I backed up too and the distance between Gib and us began to widen. The reb scout didn't know what to make of these mixed signals—we were surrendering while continuing to escape. Finally, he charged towards us with his gun still pointed in our direction.

"Now, dang-nab-it, stand still," Gib yelled in frustration. "Ya'll can't be ah given up and runnin' away at the same time."

After he had travelled another ten yards, everything became clear.

"What the…" The rest of Gib's thought trailed off as he sank angle deep in the quicksand. He managed to pull his right foot out, but the pressure on his left foot forced it deeper. He got himself half turned around, but could retreat no further. He was flailing around desperately now, a look of panic on his face. His frantic actions only made him sink faster, but he did not let go of the gun.

"Let's get up that bank so's we can get us some cover," said Eli.

"Yeah, he's madder than a hornet. We better get out of his line of fire."

By the time we reached the top of the sand ridge, the quicksand was up to Gib's knees. We laid flat so he could barely see us in our elevated position. My father had always said in any battle, he who takes the high ground has the advantage. Our position was getting more and more elevated as Gib sank into the quicksand.

"Yer gonna have ta toss that pistol a'fore we save ya," Eli shouted down to him.

"How you two tadpoles gonna save ah growned man?"

"We gotta long branch up here. We can pull ya outah thar."

"Yes, it's very sturdy," I assured him. "We used it before when I got stuck in that quicksand and it worked fine."

Gib's jaw dropped. A look of bewilderment gradually became a scowl of anger. It was not until this moment that he realized he had been set up— he had been outsmarted by a couple of kids. He twisted towards us, buried up past his knees in quicksand, and fired a shot in our direction. We quickly pulled back from the edge, and from our elevated position, he had no chance of hitting us. He was lashing out in anger.

"Ya best throw down that pistol," yelled Eli, peeking over the edge. "Less ya wantah slip under that quicksand fer ah horrible death."

"If'en the Major hears my pistol, he'll know it and will come ta save me. Then we'll skin you two whelps alive." He fired off another shot in our direction for good measure. The bullet buried itself in the sand somewhere below.

"The major is dead. You have got to believe us," I insisted. "We saw him die. There is no one else coming to your rescue. There is only us and you have to throw down your gun."

Gib struggled some more and sank deeper—now up to his waist.

"I dun told the Major goin' ta this swamp were a bad idear." He was almost sobbing now. "Nothin' ever comes ta any good inna swamp."

"Throw the gun towards us and we will get you out," I repeated.

I actually felt sorry for Gib. A half hour ago he had been bristling with swagger, a proud Confederate scout, and now he looked pathetic and scared. He panted a few quick breaths and finally threw the pistol towards us. It barely cleared the pool of quicksand. We scurried down the sand ridge with the long branch in tow. Eli got there first and picked up the gun. It was a nickel-plated navy revolver—an impressive firearm. He tried to stick the big, heavy weapon in his belt, but it was too cumbersome. Eli handed it to me, and I set it down on a clump of bristling swamp grass that had managed to grow in the sand.

"What are we going to do with him once we pull him out?" I asked. "He's not going to believe a couple of kids are actually going to shoot him."

"I'll shoot that reb fer sure," Eli declared boldly as he bent over and picked up the end of the branch. Then he let it fall again after he considered what I had said.

"Throw yerself backwards so ya spread out in the sand," Eli instructed.

Gib looked at him skeptically and instead, resumed struggling against the quicksand.

"Do it, Gib. It worked for me. It's what Dr. Shronts said to do. You won't sink any farther if you just do it."

Apparently, the advice coming from a doctor carried more weight. He threw his hands up in the air and flopped backwards into the quicksand. As he did, he was the first to notice the riders that appeared at the top of the sand ridge.

"Sarge!"

~

CHAPTER 29
To the Rescue

I followed Gib's gaze to the top of the sand ridge and saw three riders looking down on us. I held up my hand to shade my eyes from the afternoon sun. My attention was immediately draw to the huge man on a huge horse. It had to be Walter Hess, who would be the first person you would expect to volunteer to rescue two foolish boys in outlaw country.

Mr. Hess was the tallest man in town except, maybe for his son Jake; neither one of them were skinny either. He loved horses, but found few that would tolerate his weight. He rode a crossbreed that was part quarter horse and part Belgian. It was over 17 hands high and had legs like pillars.

The rider next to Hess was wearing a wide-brimmed Union officer's hat and I guessed him to be Major Carter, Libby's father. She had apparently broken her silence and told the adults of our adventure into the Grand Kankakee Marsh. *Bless her*, I thought to myself. Now I could stop fretting about what two boys such as ourselves were going to do with a full-grown outlaw once we fished him out of the quicksand. It was like the devil was in one ear telling me to leave him here to die, and an angel had the other ear saying to save this poor, misguided soul's life.

As Mr. Hess and Major Carter descended the sand ridge, it was revealed who had gotten Gib's attention. Holding up the rear was Frank—"the Sarge" to Gib.

"Frank is one of them," I yelled out.

This prompted curious looks from Mr. Hess and Major Carter. They, of course, had no idea what I was talking about.

"Shut up, Ben," said Eli. "Now he's gonna run fer it."

Indeed, he was. Frank wheeled his horse around and was about to take off back west when he took one more look at poor Gib sinking in the quicksand. Having an apparent change of heart, he turned his horse down the ridge and came up behind our two rescuers.

"Okay, gents, put up your hands," he said as he leveled his pistol on Mr. Hess and Major Carter. They looked at him in disbelief.

"Frank, what the hell are you doin'?" asked Hess.

"I'm Sergeant Frank Lester of the Army of the Confederacy," he announced proudly, his voice suddenly taking on a southern tone.

"Frank, have you taken leave of your senses?" asked Major Carter. "The war's been over more than two years now."

"Maybe fer you Yanks, but we never surrendered."

"You tell'em, Sarge," shouted Gib from his sunken position.

"Now loosen them gun belts and let them fall to the ground," he ordered. "You so much as touch yer gun butt, I'll plug ya sure."

The brows furrowed on the two men as they came to grips with the situation.

"I wondered why you came along with Major Carter and me," said Walter Hess. "You been saying for two days that going into the marsh would be a waste of time."

"Yeah," Major Carter added. "You been pestering us to turn around ever since we left Momence."

"Well, ya shoulda heeded my advice. Now unbuckle those gun belts real careful now."

Both men reluctantly did what they were told. Frank seemed to relax a little when their gun belts hit the sand.

"Sarge, them boys say the Majors done been kilt. They say it was Mike Shafer thet done it. I don't believe'um though. No one man gonna take down the Major, Bill and Skeeter in a gunfight."

Frank looked very concerned at this news. His eyes shifted from side to side as if considering what to do next.

"I don't believe them neither," he finally said, but he didn't say it with a lot of conviction. He turned his attention back to Mr. Hess and Major Carter. "Now you two get off yer horses."

Having no choice, Walter Hess and Major Carter abided. When both men dismounted, they were behind their horses. This was apparently the moment Eli was waiting for. With a movement quick as a snake, he grabbed Gib's pistol that was laying in the saw grass beside him and whirled, aimed and pulled the trigger. *Nothing happened*!

"Eli!" I shouted. "It's single action. You have to pull the hammer back first!"

As he frantically tried to pull the hammer back, it caught the attention of Gib who was stuck in the quicksand only twenty feet away.

"Sarge! Thet kid just tried ta shoot ya!"

Sergeant Frank Lester looked our way and saw Eli struggling to cock the big Navy Colt. Then I saw his gun point in our direction, the barrel flashing in the sun. My body clinched and I closed my eyes waiting for the bullet to arrive. Before Frank could pull the trigger, Walter Hess plowed into Frank and his horse with such force that the poor animal was knocked sideways and down on his haunches.

The impact sent Frank flying through the air, his arms flailing about like a deranged bird. He hit the sand so hard you could hear the air puff out of his lungs. Frank raised his head and looked around, his eyes wide open in wonder at what had just happened.

Frank was still holding his gun and, as he gathered his wits, he started to raise it in the direction of Mr. Hess as he charged towards him. A well-aimed kick from Major Carter knocked the gun from his hand. Then Walter Hess fell upon Frank and subdued him with a thunderous punch to the jaw.

"Did he kill him?" I asked.

"I hope so," said Eli.

~

CHAPTER 30
Time to Head Home

I brought back Frank's horse, which had bolted away in the excitement, and Mr. Hess threw the unconscious outlaw over the saddle. Then he took a length of rope and, reaching under the horse's belly, tied Frank's hands and feet together. It was a good bet he would not fall off with his belly over the saddle, but it didn't look too comfortable.

"What are we gonna do with him?" asked Major Carter, pointing at Gib. The reb scout was in up to his waist and looking very frightened. He had thrown himself backwards in the quicksand, so he didn't sink any farther. The sun came out from behind a cloud and began beating down on his face. His coonskin hat provided him with little protection.

"It wouldn't be Christian to leave him to die slow," said Walter Hess. "Let's pull him outah there."

I was relieved to hear this because I didn't want to head for home with the thought of Gib slowly dying in the quicksand pit. I couldn't read the expression on Eli's face, so I didn't know what his thoughts were on the matter.

"We can use that long branch over there," I suggested. "That's what they used to get me out of there."

"Ya'll hear thet! Thet thar kid got caught in here a'fore," Gib interrupted angrily to explain. "They tricked me intah steppin' in quicksand. Them two brats is the same as murderers."

Walter Hess had to laugh at this assessment. He picked up the big branch like it was a twig and extended it to Gib. The reb gratefully latched on to it and Mr. Hess pulled him out without the need for assistance. Gib's legs were a little shaky and Hess pulled him up by the scruff of the neck like a bad puppy. If he had any thoughts of escaping, he quickly abandoned them.

Eli and I went up the ridge and fetched Trooper and Mr. Tyler's filly. When we got back, Gib was slumped down in the sand. Major Carter was standing over him with a sour look on his face. "What are we going to charge this scallywag with?"

"He be part of ah gang of hoss thieves," said Eli, failing to see what the problem was.

"That's kinda vague, lad." said Major Carter. The look on his face said he was not looking for suggestions from a couple of kids.

"Eli, come on," I insisted, tugging on his shirt sleeve. "Let's go upstream while they're talking and find Gib's horse. It's probably stolen from somebody so that definitely is a specific charge."

"We can't prove it's stolen unless somebody is around to say its theirs," said Major Carter. Before the war, he was studying to become a lawyer. When he returned, that career was forgotten, but he still seemed to have a head full of legalities.

I motioned for Eli to stay on Trooper and I hopped back on the dappled-gray filly. We took off at a trot along the stagnant water beside the sand ridge. We only went a hundred yards when we heard a horse neighing. We found Gib's horse among some scrub oak tied to the thickest branch.

Next to it was Scarlett, the red pony that Gib had stolen from Doctor Shronts's place. When we rode back with Scarlett in tow, the Major looked pleasantly surprised but said nothing. Mr. Hess was more forthcoming with his praise.

"Great work boys! Now we got something more substantial to charge him with.

The possession of one Shetland pony belonging to Major John Carter of Momence, Illinois. Those judges in Kankakee like you to be specific."

"You can't take me to Kankakee," protested Gib. "We're in Indiana!"

Mr. Hess looked a bit confused and turned towards us.

"We been wandering around this marsh so long, I may have lost my bearings. We are in Illinois, aren't we boys?"

"We sure nuff are,' said Eli. This distain for proper legal procedure appealed to him.

"Damn straight we are," answered Major Carter.

"Illinois for sure," I chimed in.

"This is ah hell of ah way ta do ah man," said Gib.

This matter being properly decided, we mounted up and headed for home. Our party threaded its way down river on the left bank, dismounting several times to lead the horses through uncertain footing. After a while, I saw the makeshift sign on a stake announcing the Indiana border.

Several hours after seeing the sign, the river narrowed, and the water started moving more rapidly. We had come to the upper crossing. Watching the water spill over the rock ledge that dammed up the river, I knew home was only a mile away.

We were on what was called "Lyon's Lane", the trail that hunters and trappers followed from Momence to the Indiana wilderness. This time of year, it was deep in mud which made it difficult for the horses to walk. Eli slowed Trooper up and waited until I was next to him. There was something on his mind.

"Ya suppose Birdie is gonna be all right?" he asked.

"Who?"

"Birdie," he replied impatiently.

"Oh, yeah, ah, Mike Shafer's daughter," I stammered. "Well, I suppose so."

"I don't know. After watching Shafer kill three men like there weren't nothin' to it, I don't know. We shoulda tried ta talk her intah comin' with us."

"She wouldn't have come. You heard her. She didn't want to leave her mother there alone with him."

Eli considered this a moment and said nothing. He looked like he had just swallowed a bitter pill. I decided I might as well hit him with what was bothering me.

"Are we going to tell them about Mike Shafer killing those three men?"

"Don't see no need. They ain't gonna arrest Mike Shafer for killin' three Confederate outlaws. They might want to give him a medal. If'en Gib brings it up, we might have to fess up. Don't think he will though."

"You're probably right, but it seems like we should tell someone about it."

"If'en we do, then they'll know we went to Shafer's place to get those hosses back and they'll be thinkin' we're plumb loco. Liable ta lock us up in one of those places fer crazy folks."

I suppose that makes sense, but it didn't sit well with me. It seemed like someone should know. *But who?* They were three raiding Confederates fighting a lost cause. How many other men had died in the war and their relatives would never know their fate?

"Town's up ahead," shouted back Major Carter.

It sure enough was a wonderful sight to see after days in the wilderness. We had made it home by sunset, but barely. There were golden rays of sunlight cutting through the leaves as darkness closed in. Even in the dim light of dusk, Momence, Illinois had never looked so good to me.

"You boys are gonna have to be answering a lot of questions," said Walter Hess, as he dropped back to talk to us. "We have a newspaper now—The Momence Reporter. I'm sure Mr. Paradis, the editor, will have some questions for you."

"Oh, we don't want no fuss bein' made," said Eli.

"Too late for that. You fellas pulled off quite a stunt, going out to Bogus Island and bringing those horses back after the sheriff refused to go. I, for one, am damn sure impressed. I thought I had some sand when I was your age, but I woulda never done something like this. You boys got some grit."

Major Carter did not appear to share Mr. Hess's enthusiasm for our adventure. He was giving us long looks and nipping on his pocket flask. The cheery mood he was in when we brought back Libby's pony had faded. He was deep in his cups, as my father used to say, and taking a dim view of everything around him.

"Where is Libby's canoe?" he asked. "Her grandfather made that for her with his own two hands."

"Ah, well, the canoe is safe, sir," I assured him. "It's at Dr. Shront's cabin. We'll go back and get it as soon as we can."

"I doubt your mother will let you out of her sight after this stunt."

Somehow, when Mr. Hess called it a "stunt", it sounded better than when Major Carter borrowed the term. Me and Eli preferred to think of it as an adventure. Somebody told me an adventure was something dangerous you did and loved to talk about, but you would never want to do again.

I was glad that the Major was directing all his spite towards me. I am sure he considers Eli some "wild child" from the lower class. It would be easy to blame him and that would not be fair; this whole thing had been my idea.

~

CHAPTER 31
No Rest at Home

"**Y**ou are not to leave your room today," said my mother in as strict a voice as she could muster. She was standing at the door of my bedroom with her arms folded in a stance that told me she was serious.

"Am I going to get anything to eat?" I was hoping starvation wasn't part of the punishment. Four days in the marsh on short rations had peaked my appetite.

"Well, of course you will. I will bring up your lunch at noon and allow you to come down for dinner at six o'clock."

I could tell my mother was trying to be tough, but she was wavering. Me and Eli had brought back Trooper, Mr. Tyler's filly and Libby's red pony when no adult had volunteered to go to Bogus Island. No lawsuit from Mr. Tyler and more importantly, we had exposed Frank as part of the gang. Mother was so relieved that I don't think she would have punished me at all if it hadn't been for Major Carter. He was real happy out in the marsh when we rode up with Scarlett. As he sipped from his flask on the way home, he stopped

217

looking at the bright side and became upset about us taking Libby's canoe and leaving it. By the time he brought me home at ten o'clock, he was telling my mother I needed to be punished for my reckless behavior.

"You know Major Carter is right, don't you? Leaving with no permission and telling no one was a very irresponsible thing to do. I know it was probably Eli that put you up to this, but you still need to be punished. I still don't know why your father was so partial to that boy."

"It was my idea. I talked Eli into it. I would have surely died out there if it weren't for him."

She considered this as she stood there, her fingers running up and down the frame of the door as if she were playing the piano. "Well, ah, I don't know," she concluded, still standing in the doorway as though she had something else to say but couldn't get it out.

"At least Frank's on his way to jail," I said, taking a guess as to what was on her mind.

"Yes, I will be eternally grateful to you for exposing Frank as a fraud. I know I should have never been taken in by his charms."

"Don't feel bad. Frank is a skilled con man. He studied Dad's letters to find out about our family. He talked like somebody born and raised in Illinois."

"It's just that it has been so hard for me after your father died. Before the war, we were well off. We saw the Carters and other prominent families socially on a regular basis. Now all that has changed. I'm forced to work teaching school and doing other things to make ends meet. It's just been very hard for me to adjust."

"Yes, with all that is going on, it was understandable you misjudged Frank."

"I guess I wanted so badly for Frank to be the man he pretended to be."

"Well, he wasn't and he's gone now."

"I just want you to promise you will not do anything like this again. I thought I had lost you. I didn't sleep for three nights. I can't lose you. I have already lost your father. I can't lose you too."

She gave a little shudder, barely getting the last words out, and then she began to cry.

Then a different viewpoint of what I had done hit me like a punch in the gut. I was so wrapped up in putting together the plan, so intent on proving the adults wrong, that I had not even left a note. I tried to imagine myself as a parent. What would I have done

if my child had vanished for four days without a word. I wondered if all kids my age
were this selfish or was it just me.

"I'm sorry I worried you Mother."

~

CHAPTER 32
Yet Another Visitor

A pebble hit my window early this morning and awakened me. It was Eli waving good-bye. He had to get back to Hopkins Park to care for his grandfather. Eli had spent the night in the bunkhouse in the stable. It is where he had slept for most of his young life when his grandfather worked for us. He was moved out when Frank came into our lives. Now Frank was gone, awaiting trial in Kankakee, and hopefully things would return to normal. The bunkhouse would be there for Eli any time he could get away from his responsibilities in Hopkin's Park. I usually slipped down the drainpipe on those occasions and stayed out there with him.

Walter Hess had turned Frank over to the local constable for transportation to Kankakee for trial. I could not imagine the ex-Confederate con man getting off with a light sentence. Gib, whose full name was James Gibson, was facing twenty years for the theft of a Shetland pony. Mr. Hess said he was lucky Illinois was an enlightened state; we didn't hang horse thieves any-more.

As I laid there contemplating the con-versation I had just had with my mother, another pebble hit my window. *This is be-coming a regular thing.* This one almost broke the glass. I opened the window and leaned out the sash. It was a boy I didn't rec-ognize. Then Libby turned her face upward towards me. She was in her boy duds; the torn shirt and worn pants I had given her for when she wanted to be a Tomboy.

"Ben, can you come down so we can talk?" she asked in what was a very loud whisper. Luckily my mother was next door delivering Mrs. Osborn's laundry. She never brought it up that she was doing laundry to make ends meet. I never mentioned it ei-ther, but I knew.

"I can't leave my room. It's my punish-ment for running off into the marsh without permission."

I was about to tell her I would come down anyway, but she had already grabbed ahold of the drainpipe and was climbing in my direction.

"Libby, what are you doing?"

"Isn't this how Eli gets up to your room?"

"Yeah, but..."

She had already scaled the drainpipe and was leaning in towards me.

"Well, help me in."

I grabbed her arm and yanked her through the window. Our cheeks pressed together for an instant as I hauled her in and she landed on top of me. Our noses were almost touching as we looked at each other for a long, awkward moment before she rolled off of me. We had wrestled with each other before when we were younger, but it had never produced the strange sensation that it did this time.

Libby sat on the floor in front of me and crossed her legs. She leaned forward with a serious look on her face.

"Benjamin, I want to apologize for the way my father treated you last night. It was a brave and foolish thing that you and Eli did—very foolish, but your heart was in the right place. He had no right to be yelling at you for being irresponsible. He is the last person that should be talking about being irresponsible with his drinking and all. If it wasn't for my grandfather running things, we would have lost everything already."

"But he was sorta right, Libby. I didn't know what I was putting my mother through. She didn't sleep for the three nights I was gone. And I put Eli up to this. Your dad wanted to pin this on him because he thinks Eli is some kind of wild child, but it was my idea."

"Yes, both my parents are very concerned about everyone being in their proper place in society."

"Since you brought up being proper, how did you get out of the house in those hand-me-down clothes I gave you?"

"Slid down the drainpipe. Same way I'm leaving here."

"Isn't your mother trying to arrange some kind of fancy coming out party for you? You'll be a debutante. Real high society stuff will come to Momence. You know, like you'll dress up with a corsette and have a ten-layer dress."

"It's more like a dress and six petticoats and it's not going to happen if I can help it."

"You should have never read those stories by A.M. Barnard. That's where you got the idea of dressing up like a boy."

"Louisa May Alcott is coming out with a book all about four sisters and she is using her own name."

"What? Are you saying A. M. Barnard is really a woman?"

"Yes, A.M. Barnard is the pen name of Louisa May Alcott. She is a transcendentalist and knows Henry David Thoreau and Ralph Waldo Emerson. "

"Oh." I let this revelation sink in for a minute.

"I have to go now." Libby was out the window and down the drainpipe before I could ask her what a transcendentalist was. That word was really a mouthful.

People have said I have a gift for learning, but I can't hold a candle to Libby. If she wasn't a girl, she could probably become a famous professor or lawyer or something like that.

~

CHAPTER 33
The Entry Fee

There was already a crowd gathered outside the barn next to Binder's Harness Shop when Eli and I arrived. There were sporting men who were strangers to our town milling around flashing money. The word of the big race had spread.

We worked our way through the crowd, gradually making our way to the wide-open doors of the barn. There were other kids hanging around to see what was going on; townies who were now off for the summer and bored, looking for some excitement. Unfortunately, I ran into my tormenters since second grade—the Van der Wick twins—Harold and Henry.

"What are you doing here, Benjy?" asked Henry, a sneer on his lips.

"Why aren't you sitting up in your bedroom readin' ah book?" asked Harold, giving me a push.

"Hey, ah, don't do that," I protested.

"What ya gonna do about it, bookworm?"

The harassment ended immediately when Eli appeared by my side.

"Beat it, you two goobers."

Without another word, the Van der Wick twins turned around and melted into the crowd.

This was not the first time Eli had saved me from Henry and Harold. I was about to thank him for running off the twins, but he cut me off with an announcement: "You gotta do the talkin' in here."

"What?"

"You're the son of a war hero and you're white. They ain't gonna pay no attention to me."

This was not what I wanted to hear. I had just been intimidated by the Van der Wick twins. I was not feeling very confident. Now I'm supposed to walk into this barn full of grown men and announced I wanted in the race.

When we finally worked our way into the barn, there was a lively discussion going on between Jim Johnson, the race's unofficial organizer, and a trapper named Larue Mauvois.

"There weren't no word got out 'bout any entry fee," Larue complained.

"It was on the handbills that were handed out," said Johnson, holding one out for Larue to inspect.

"It's in English," said Larue. "I only read French."

"That ain't my fault."

Larue Mauvois told people he was a trapper, but his trips into the wilderness were becoming less frequent as he busied himself more and more with the sporting crowd in the taverns in town. My father knew him from before and had once said Larue was a man without virtue or morals.

As Larue frowned and scratched his beard, not liking what he was hearing, a portly man I only knew as Spike blocked our view.

"What you boys doin' in here? Can't ya see this here is man talk?"

"We wanta get in the race," said Eli firmly.

"You can't get in the race. You're just a couple of kids."

"But we need the money real bad." I blurted this out not thinking how ridiculous it would sound. Times were hard and everybody needed money real bad.

Then Eli tried to go around Spike and the hefty man shoved him back. Eli quickly regained his balance, but Spike had pushed him into aging Mr. Prescott. The old man lost his balance and fell, his cane flying in Johnson's direction.

"Hey, what's going on there?" asked the race organizer.

"I was just tryin' ta get these kids outah here, Jim. Didn't mean ta knock down Mr. Prescott."

"What're you kids doin' in here?" demanded Johnson.

Eli nudged me and I knew it was my time to step forward.

"We want to enter the race, sir." I tried to say it as resolutely as possible, but my voice cracked a little at the end.

My request was greeted with a round of laughter.

"Why sure you can enter the race," said Johnson with a broad grin. "There is one spot left assuming Mr. Mauvois is going to stop complaining and ponies up. So there might be two. Just give me your fifty dollars in cash for the entry fee."

"Fifty dollars!" Eli and I let out in unison.

"Yes, what do you think Mr. Mauvois has been complaining about?"

With Spike trying so hard to throw us out, we missed the fifty-dollar part. No wonder Mauvois was putting up a stink. Fifty dollars was a sizeable sum to risk considering the average working man made less than a dollar a day.

"That is a hefty amount of money," I said. "Why so much?".

"Here's the way we're doing it. Ten riders put in fifty each and that's five hundred. Then the race backers will match it with five hundred. That's where the thousand-dollar prize is coming from."

Walking in here, I knew our chances of getting in the race were slim. This was like a punch in the gut.

"We don't got that kind ah money," Eli said and tugged on my collar to go.

"You gotta prime the pump in order to receive," said Johnson. He motioned with his head for Spike to usher us out of the stable. The fat man looked eager to do just that.

"I'll put up their entry fee," said a deep voice. Everyone kind of froze in place as the huge figure of Jake Hess stepped forward.

"Well, that's a generous offer, Jake," said Jim Johnson, "but why, ah, ...not that I'm questioning you."

"Let's say I have an interest in their horse."

Truth be told, Jake Hess did have an interest in Trooper. He wanted to buy him and had made an offer of three hundred dollars last month. With Old Shaf's hatred of the Hess family, this is where the rumor started that the outlaw was behind the theft.

Jim Johnson was scratching his chin, trying to think of some reason not to let us in the race. "Whose gonna ride the horse, Jake? They're a couple of kids."

"I'm gonna ride Trooper," Eli stepped forward and declared. "I been ridin' him fer years."

Jim Johnson looked at Eli narrowly. "Ain't you from Hopkins Park? You're a ..."

"He's a what?' challenged Jake Hess sternly.

Johnson looked up at the towering young man and squeaked out, "I guess it's alright."

"Mon Dieu, I will be racing against children," declared Larue. "I can not lose."

As the crowd began to thin now that all the race positions were spoken for, we worked our way over to Jake Hess. He was talking to a couple of men, but broke away and came over to us.

"Make me proud," he said. "I've seen that stallion run."

"Thank you, sir." I was stumbling for the right words.

"But why did ya put up money fer us?" asked Eli.

"Let's just say my father, Walter, is an admirer of you two. He says you remind him of himself when he was young. He likes your grit."

~

CHAPTER 34
Race Day

The race was set to go off at 11 o'clock, but me and Eli arrived early because we wanted to get the lay of the land. Several other riders were already there. The thousand-dollar purse was a reason for extra preparation. Riders were wiping down their horses and double-checking equipment. There was a nervous excitement in the air.

Most were familiar participants at the horse races on the road west of town. The races were usually a quarter mile straight away and the quickly accelerating quarter horse ruled. Although previous race winners were full of confidence, this one-mile race would be a different game.

"You know why Jake Hess is backin' us, don't ya?" asked Eli.

"He likes us, I guess."

"Yeah, and we got a good shot here. Trooper's sire was a thoroughbred. Better in a long race."

I do remember my father putting in a lot of time studying the characteristics of different breeds. The stud for Trooper was a thoroughbred from the Highland Stock Farm in Beecher, Illinois.

The arrival of Bob Hoskin from Bourbonnais Grove caused a stir. He was a competitive little man known for having a short fuse. He had not even dismounted before he was in a confrontation with Jim Johnson, the race organizer.

"Hey, Jimmy! What the hell kind of track is this? We gotta ride a half mile and turn around and come back. Just make it a straight away! You wanta do something like this, build an oval track like in New York."

"This ain't New York and we can't afford to build an oval track. They're gonna build one down in Louisville. Wait and go race there."

"Yeah, Jim. Why don't ya throw up a few fences and we'll have us a steeple chase," added a man name Watson. He was riding a sturdy little quarter horse that had won a race last year.

"This is the best we could do. A couple of the upright members of the council ain't particular fans of this race and won't let us extend the raceway beyond the crossing. Say we'll be a danger to people passing through."

Watson waved his hand to dismiss this answer and rode over to the starting line.

Eli was listening to all these complaints and gave me his opinion.

"I don't think that turn around the hay wagon down there is gonna hurt our chances none. Trooper can turn on a dime and give ya ten cents change."

The hay wagon he was referring to was a half a mile down the road and piled high with straw. It was the point the racers would pivot and return to the start. Johnson had men construct a crude grandstand out of wooden planks. It was quickly filling up as spectators gathered to watch the high stakes contest.

Several of the area's sporting men were working the crowd, dollar bills in their hand, covering bets on who would be the winner. The most well-known was a man from Chicago called Sweeny who always wore a top hat and a diamond stickpin in his expensive tie. He covered the big bets and there would be some for this well-advertised event.

All turned in the direction of Larue Mauvois, the favorite, when he made his noisy entrance. He was riding a big horse he called Napoleon, part thoroughbred like Trooper, and good for distance. In the past year, the longest race was one half mile and Napoleon had won.

"Larue, you are going off at two ta one," yelled a bearded bet maker. "Can't make no money betting on you."

"Do not complain, mon ami. You'll double yer money and it's a sure thing. They made me put up fifty of my own money. No way I intend to lose this."

I was listening to this exchange as Eli was kneeling, rubbing down Trooper's forelegs.

"He sounds pretty sure of himself."

"What?" asked Eli, looking up.

"Larue, he says there is no way he will lose. They have him at two to one odds."

"What are the odds on us?"

"I don't know. Probably not good. Who's going to bet on a couple of kids?"

Someone blew a horn that signaled for the riders to move to the starting line. I led Trooper with Eli on board. As always, he was riding bareback. He had been riding Trooper that way since the horse was a two-year-old. Eli's long legs were very good for clinging to the big stallion.

"Good luck," I said, looking up at him. He looked tense but determined.

"Don't need luck," Eli replied. "Ya better get outah here fer ya get stepped on."

The starting line was becoming dangerous as the nine other riders tried to maneuver for position. Jim Johnson was walking back and forth waving his starting pistol, waiting for all the horses to be facing forward and still behind the line. When that moment happened, he raised the gun and fired.

"They're off!"

~

CHAPTER 35
A Dangerous Ride

It was a fast start. Mauvois's horse jumped sideways out of the gate and ran into a farm boy's horse knocking him out of his saddle. The young man was a favorite to win. By the time he righted himself, he was ten yards behind the pack. Hopefully it was an unintended accident; it was hard to tell with Larue Mauvois. He had a reputation for doing anything necessary to win.

I ran down the side of the road with my father's binoculars, trying to find some place where I could see the whole race. I ran right through a bunch of folks from Hopkins Park who were here to cheer on Eli and a negro jockey called Little Nick. He was older than Eli and more experienced. Before the war, he had ridden in races down south where most of the jockeys in this dangerous line of work were slaves. Small and light, Little Nick was working the quarter horse he was riding towards the head of the pack.

I spotted a solitary oak tree along the raceway with a bough I was able to jump up and reach. I pulled myself up and straddled the hefty limb. As I brought my father's old field glasses to my eyes, the riders were already approaching the tricky turning point that was a half a mile away. They had covered the hay wagon with straw to make the turn wider or in case someone ran into it. I don't know the actual reason, but it looked like a bright yellow hill in the middle of the road.

Little Nick had taken the lead with Hoskins right on his tail. Mauvois was a close third followed by Eli on Trooper. It made little difference because the only thing that mattered was how they came out of the tight turn.

I could see Hoskin's move coming before he made it. He was on the inside of Little Nick and pushed him wide as they made the turn. The devious maneuver cost him because, as he forced Little Nick to the outside, it slowed him enough that Mauvois slipped by him on the inside. As I refocused the binoculars, I imagined I could see the wily smile on Larue Mauvois's face. If it was there, it wasn't for long.

As he had promised, Eli proved he was best in the tight turn. He came so close to the wagon, straw was flying up on the track. When Mauvois looked back, Eli was half a length back and gaining on him. I could see the Frenchman taking the whip to his horse, but Trooper was still gaining on him. When Eli was about to pass him on the outside, Mauvois tried to push Eli into the ditch of the roadway, but Napoleon didn't have any interest in bouncing into Trooper, a bigger horse. When this didn't work, the angry Frenchman swung his riding crop at Eli. He ducked the first swing, but the next one must have hit him—*Eli disappeared*!

"Oh, no," I screamed, throwing my arms in the air. Off balance, I fell out of the tree. Hitting the ground knocked the wind out of me. When I got up and dusted myself off, it hit me. *What happened*? I looked around frantically for my binoculars. When I found them, I focused on where Eli disappeared. He wasn't on the roadway. Was he in the ditch? Hopefully a softer landing.

I ran towards where I last saw Eli, a quarter mile away. I ignored the cheers at the finish line. How were these adults ignoring the fate of a fourteen-year-old boy? Like the end of a battle, the winners cheering and walking by the bodies of their dead. Why didn't they consider the price of winning?

~

CHAPTER 36
The Finish Line

When I got to the place where Eli disappeared, I found no limp body lying in the ditch. Totally confused, I looked towards the cheers coming my way from the finish line. I still had the binoculars in my hand and raised them to my eyes. What I saw was a shock and a relief. Eli was riding around on the big shoulders of Jake Hess as the crowd cheered!

I ran flat out for a quarter mile to the finish line. When I got there, I was so out of breath I could barely get out my question. "What happened?"

"The kid won!" shouted Jim Johnson, the race organizer.

"How?" I managed to get out, my hands grasping my knees as I tried to catch my breath. Johnson was already yelling at someone else, and I couldn't get his attention again. Then I got another surprise. Libby emerged from the crowd and grabbed me by the shoulders.

"You guys did it, Ben! You won!" She pulled me towards her and gave me a kiss right on the lips. This sent my head spinning. She was in the boy's duds I had given her and her hair was up under a slouch hat. Two men standing nearby gave us long looks, but I didn't care. I had so many different feelings bouncing around my head, I sat down, afraid to walk any farther. As I sat there, letting everything sink in, it came over me like a wave. I didn't even have a word for it, but Mr. Trowbridge would. I searched for it through the list of difficult spelling words he challenged us with. *Euphoria!* That was it. I was overwhelmed with happiness.

"Ben, are you alright?" Libby was bending over with her hand on my shoulder and a concerned look on her face. I looked up and said, "I'm fine." I knew I had a stupid, silly smile my face, but I didn't care.

"Did you see it?" she asked. "It was amazing!"

"What?"

"That Mauvois guy started swinging his whip at Eli and he disappeared. When Trooper got a half a length ahead of Mauvois's horse, Eli reappeared like magic. He had slipped around and was clinging to Trooper's side. He said that's what Indians did out west when soldiers were shooting at them. Everyone went crazy when they saw him again. He beat Mauvois by a length."

Libby's description jogged my memory. I remembered Eli doing this tricky maneuver last year and scaring the heck out of me. How was I to know it would come in handy later?

There was a commotion behind me, and I turned around to see Mauvois had found a new use for his whip. There was a bunch of men trying to pull him off his horse and he was keeping them at bay with the riding crop. Some were yelling to arrest him, and others wanted to lynch him. He whirled his horse in a circle and rode away.

"Good riddance," said Libby. "He is a horrible man."

I thought of Mike Shafer and the fate of the ex-Confederates. I now had a different view of what a horrible man was.

"Let's find Eli," I said.

"That won't be easy."

The group of men surrounding the winner of the thousand-dollar one mile race was starting to dwindle. A few unhappy souls passed us, mumbling about losing their money betting on anyone but us. I guess that was understandable.

"Hey Eli, you did it," I grabbed his hand and shook it like a pump handle. He was all smiles.

"Ben, Libby, we won! I told ya nobody could beat Trooper in ah mile run."

We did a group hug while jumping up and down. We were so excited, we didn't notice some old friends that had approached us.

"Congratulations," said Doctor John Shronts.

"Ya'll done it," said Sam Patch, who was at the doctor's side.

"You don't know it," said the doctor, "but I was trying to turn you two over to the sheriff to bring you back before you embarked on this foolhardy venture. I'm glad that it all worked out for you."

I looked at Eli and he gave me a sly smile. *Oh, we knew it.* Had he forgotten that we snuck out of his cabin before dawn?

"Thank you, Doctor Shronts," was my only reply.

"How'd ya get here?" asked Eli. I was curious too.

"We brought the canoe back."

"Yeah, even with my leg in ah cast it was easy," said Sam. "Going downriver with the current, I didn't have ta paddle much at all. Easy peasy."

"I came by horseback trailing Sam's horse," said the doctor. "He might not find riding back with his cast that easy, but we will make it."

"What about Gray Wolf?" I asked. "Have you seen him?"

"Yes, he came over and told us to wish you well."

"I asked him ta come along," said Sam, "but he said too many white men."

We all got a chuckle out of that response. I thought of the old mare that we had given him. Surprisingly, my mother had not even asked about Maggie. I guess nobody places a lot of value on a horse up in years. It all worked out though because she was a good partner for the last of the Shawnee.

I saw Jake Hess approaching and pulled on Eli's sleeve to get his attention.

"Here comes Mr. Hess," I said. "Should we be giving him half the prize money or something?"

"I suppose. We wouldn't ta been in the race if'un he didn't put up the fifty dollars."

When Jake Hess walked up to us, we had to crane our necks to look up at the big man.

He was standing there smiling like a proud favorite uncle.

"That was a great ride," he exclaimed in his booming voice. "You fellas pulled it off. Now I understand why my father wanted to back you. He couldn't come down here because, being a leading citizen, he's got to be officially against gambling."

"So what do we owe him fer backin' us?" Eli got right to the point.

"Oh, nothing. You fellas keep all the money. You earned it."

"We need to at least pay him the fifty back," I said.

"No, I got that all covered. You keep the whole purse."

"But, ah..." I stammered.

"I said don't worry about it. I bet a hundred dollars on you with Sweeny at ten to one. I got a thousand coming he owes me. Sweeny is crying poor, but I will get the money out of him. I told him to sell that big diamond stickpin."

THE END

EPILOGUE

The novel *The Outlaw Islands* is historical fiction which means the fictional characters were interacting with real historical figures. Here is what is known of the later lives of these actual people.

In March of 1869, the criminal career of Mike Shafer came to a violent end. The word came over the state line that he had been shot in the back as he was entering his cabin. The outlaw was living alone at the time, his wife having passed away. Before she died, she had convinced her surviving daughter that she had to leave. A sympathetic Justice of the Peace named Coffelt had a young man escort her south beyond the Wabash River. She was never heard from again. (I like to think that young man was named Eli). It should be noted that soon after providing this help, Mr. Coffelt had nine head of livestock poisoned. "Old Shaf" never let a slight go unpunished.

Doctor John F. Shronts performed the autopsy on Mike Shafer and plucked enough buckshot out of his body to kill three men. I guess the assassin knew what his fate would be if he only wounded Old Shaf. Dr. Shronts was often called upon to treat the outlaws on Bogus Island. He was blindfolded so he could not reveal the location of the outlaw's hidden underwater bridge to the island.

In 1873, Lemuel Milk, the largest landowner in Illinois, decided to cash in his ownership of Beaver Lake. Digging the ditch wider and deeper, they had what his daughter referred to as "the opening of the waters." As they clicked champagne glasses, the dam was opened, and Beaver Lake poured into the "big ditch." Thousands of fish flopped around helplessly and died. Buffalo died slowly as they became mired in the mud and could not escape. Ducklings not yet able to fly died covered with sludge. The smell was horrible and if the wind blew from the east, the odor of death reached Momence.

A few years later, Milk's daughter Jenny was deeded the land for a dollar, and she began renting the 16,000 acres of lake bottom to share croppers. Jenny was an ambitious lady and founded her own town, Conrad, which disappeared over the years, but travelling north on route 41, a person can still see a stone marker of its location.

Walter Hess and his son Jake remained in Momence and were vital to the development of the community.

As for Bogus Island, it became a giant sand hill after the lake was drained. Indiana put that sand to good use, hauling it away to make the roadbed for route 41. Today there is a big sign along the road that points out where the island used to be. Off in the distance you can see what remains of the infamous outlaw hangout. It is now an observation point in the Kankakee Sands Nature Conservatory to view the rejuvenated buffalo herd. Please visit there and imagine what used to be.

~~~

Made in the USA
Monee, IL
10 May 2024

58054677R00152